Eva Hanagan was b Highlands of Scotland. the Foreign Office staff Vienna for four years. She married an Army officer and life as a Service wife took her to Germany and the Middle East. They have two sons, and since her husband John's retirement from the Army they have lived in Sussex.

Also by Eva Hanagan

ALICE

IN THRALL

PLAYMATES

THE UPAS TREE

HOLDING ON

A KNOCK AT THE DOOR

THE
DAISY
ROCK

~

Eva Hanagan

WARNER BOOKS

A *Warner* Book

First published in Great Britain in 1998
by Warner Books

Copyright © Eva Hanagan 1998

The extract from *The Complete Poems of D H Lawrence* is
reproduced by kind permission of Laurence Pollinger Ltd and
the Estate of Frieda Lawrence Ravagli.

The moral right of the author has been asserted.

All characters in this publication are fictitious and any
resemblance to real persons, living or dead, is purely coincidental.

A CIP catalogue record for this book is
available from the British Library.

ISBN 0 7515 2150 7

Typeset in Ehrhardt by M Rules
Printed and bound in Great Britain by
Clays Ltd, St Ives plc

Warner Books
A Division of
Little, Brown and Company (UK)
Brettenham House
Lancaster Place
London WC2E 7EN

For Maggie

1
~

'Christ, woman – keep away from the bally window!' Fergus shouted. So Flora opened the back door instead, but only a crack, her hand gripping the knob ready to push the door shut if he should look round again. But it was unlikely that he would turn his head now, not when the blades were poised within two inches . . . one inch . . . of their objective.

Flora could see his tongue protruding below his moustache. Ought she to call out to him, advise him to withdraw it? If there really should be an explosion there was the risk that his teeth might automatically clamp. But to distract his attention now, surely that would be foolish, dangerous.

Dangerous? Flora let her breath go, the awareness that she had been holding it shaming her into the realisation that she had, if only momentarily, permitted herself to share his fantasy. And who, she asked herself with growing

1

irritation, is going to empty the earth out of the dustbin and tidy everything away when this pantomime is over? Meanwhile the wind was blowing the decanted rubbish all over the lawn.

The long-handled pruner edged a fraction forward. Fergus bent his knees and crouched down behind the parapet of peat-filled plastic sacks. I'm not going to watch, Flora assured herself, but she did not retreat from her vantage point. The whole thing is too ridiculous! He can't possibly believe it either – that that brown envelope embedded in the soil packed into the dustbin actually contains an explosive device! Her guess was that it held a box of wedding-cake; although who might be sending Fergus such a thing she couldn't imagine. It might be an Old Boy, there might be some who still observed such conventions. But to date there had been no evidence that Fergus occupied a place, affectionate or otherwise, in the memories of his ex-pupils.

He was actually sweating! She could see glistening droplets trickling down his forehead and losing themselves in the thicket of his grey eyebrows.

Snip. Flora closed her eyes. Snip. A soft thud; Flora raised her eyelids. One of the sacks had slid to the ground. Fergus was waving the pruner, the slit envelope dangled, upside down now, from one of its parted blades.

A neat, shining packet, instantly recognisable, slid harmlessly to the ground.

*

Flora was standing at the sink vigorously drying the breakfast crockery when Fergus came in. His trousers were dark-patched from kneeling on the damp grass, his shirt had worked loose from the waistband at the back, and his bushy white hair had been blown into a cockatoo crest. Please God, let him laugh, then everything will be all right.

He tossed an opened cigarette pack on to the table. 'It could very well be a try-on. Put one off one's guard! Then, next time—'

'But it says "free introductory offer" on the pack, dear.'

'Ah, but I didn't send off for it, did I? Not a brand I've ever smoked.' Fergus looked critically at the cigarette between his fingers. 'Quite pleasant, though.' He replaced it between his lips and took a long reflective pull. 'Rum business, very rum!'

'Honestly! I ask you, Fergus, who on earth would . . . and, anyway, why you?'

'The way things are nowadays – well, there's no knowing, is there?' Fergus had seated himself at the kitchen table and, chair tilted perilously, was staring at the ceiling, eyes narrowed behind the cigarette smoke.

One of these fine days he's going to tip over backwards and catch his head such a crack – that'll give him something real to think about! Flora could feel a prickling at the back of her eyes, incipient tears; but whether of pity or exasperation she did not know.

3

The letter which had also arrived by the early post was still where he had carelessly thrust it, in the breast pocket of his shirt. Fergus raised his arms and clasped his hands behind his head. The envelope edged a little higher and Flora could see that it was from Stella – her neat incisive handwriting was unmistakeable. The letter would be addressed to both of them, but that Fergus would regard as a polite formality which in no way affected his right to be the one first to read it. Fergus habitually read his sister's letters twice over before tossing them to Flora. The second reading, she suspected, was cursory, its real purpose being to give him time to compose a suitably caustic comment.

'The men came this morning to empty the bin. All that rubbish on the lawn . . .' Flora's voice tailed away. Fergus gave no indication that he had heard her or, indeed, that he was even aware that she stood there twisting the damp teacloth in her hands.

Impatiently she flung the cloth on the table and banged the door behind her as she went out to the garden. She stood still for a moment, listening for the thud of his chair as he righted it or for the sound of his step as he came to join her; but there was only silence.

It was not only anger and resentment that boosted her energy and lent speed to her efforts to restore tidiness to the lawn but also a sudden anxiety that Mr Hazel might emerge at any moment for his customary after-breakfast saunter. How could she explain, Flora asked herself, feverishly dismantling the bulwark of peat sacks. Not, of course, that Mr Hazel would ask any questions. No, he would just glance over the hedge, raise his prissy straw hat and make some remark about the weather. But he would wonder – well, anyone would! Fergus maintained that only the socially insecure worried about what a neighbour might think. Oh, damn Fergus!

The final trip with the wheelbarrow accomplished, the last of the bags stacked once more with their fellows by the side of the potting shed, Flora slowly straightened her back and was glad that no one could witness the accompanying grimace. Only the lawn with its edging of flower beds lay immediately behind Hillcrest, the greater part of the garden lay at right angles to the house. Flora, allowing her glance, against her better judgement, to sweep across its expanse, reflected that it was an arrangement that had its advantages – not the least being that the garden's presence, far less its state, did not impinge upon one's conscience every time one looked out of a window.

A greenhouse, neglected, has an air of squalor particularly its own, thought Flora, staring with detachment at that structure. '*And* there's a greenhouse!' Fergus had enthused. 'The old Wing-Co used to grow more tomatoes and cucumbers than he could use. Sold the surplus and that paid for the fertilisers and so forth.' That horticultural success had doubtless been achieved while his wife was still alive, thought Flora with wry insight. Oh well, bully for the Wing-Co now cosily installed in his service flat. But the greenhouse had its merits, she conceded, making her way over the uneven flagstoned path to its warm shelter.

She hauled a rickety deckchair from under the staging and set it up in the narrow gangway. Disturbed by her intrusion, a cloud of white fly rose from the tomato plants and hung briefly on the air, light as drifting woodash. Mindful of the woodworm which infested its frame, Flora lowered herself gingerly on to the chair's mildewed canvas.

It was getting on for midday. Fergus would be pottering about with his aquarium – his *marine* aquarium; Fergus was concerned to make the distinction clear.

It seemed to Flora that when Fergus had decided to keep fish he had opted to acquire the salt-water variety in the belief that that held a certain cachet. Ordinary aquaria, or so Fergus maintained, had acquired suburban or institutional associations. Besides, the management of a marine aquarium demanded more skill and care. Certainly his aquarium had proved to provide great scope for obsessive, time-consuming activity. Today, being a Wednesday, Fergus would be making his weekly test of the salinity of the water in the tank – peering at the hydrometer, cautiously adding fresh rain-water until the reading was precisely 1.025. A little cube of the reeking bloodworms and tiny shrimps which he insisted on storing in the freezer would already be thawing out on the draining board in readiness for the twice daily feeding ritual. But next Wednesday, being the fourth in the monthly cycle, he would siphon out a third of the water and replace it with buckets of water which had been previously brought, with the maximum of fuss, to the required temperature and correct salinity. A trail of damp patches between the scullery sink, the kitchen and the sitting room would bear witness to his labours.

Instead of being irritated, I ought to feel grateful that Fergus has an absorbing interest; two interests, really, if one includes golf, Flora told herself, scratching half-heartedly at a nettle sting on her leg while she waited for the sensation of gratitude which failed to materialise.

Positive thinking, she decided, seemed to elude her this morning. She had more success in cultivating that approach to life in the Spring. It was evident that late September was more conducive to a melancholy mood. But one need not allow one's humour to be determined by such considerations; and I don't. Or, at least, not as a rule, Flora assured herself.

After all, there were days – and they were not only confined to the Spring, she reminded herself – when, in defiance of all logic, she just knew that something lovely was about to happen; that life was really going to begin, whatever that might mean. She did wonder if she was unique in possessing that capacity for hope, that sense that for the present one was merely marking time, wait-ing for the coming of tomorrow . . . next week . . . next year, when everything would be quite, quite different. But without that feeling, deprived of that instinct, how could people go on living?

That nonsense that Fergus had got up to this morning, that was no more than his way of injecting a little excitement into his life. It would be pointless to allow herself to worry over it – in any case, what could she do about it? People had different ways of . . . in any event, surely Fergus's antics were no more childish than her own daydreaming?

Was it having children that made things easier for some people, reconciled them to the fact that while their own lives might not have come up to expectation, their offspring might somehow succeed where the parents had failed? Being a parent might, of itself, lend purpose and meaning to one's life; make it less likely that one would be plagued by the whisper of that inner voice which asked not only what one had achieved in life but also what, if anything, had been expected of one.

If their child had survived, life might have been very different, thought Flora. There were times, no matter how hard she tried to refrain from such thoughts, when Flora found herself speculating about what her daughter would have been like had she grown up; by now she would have been a woman in her mid-thirties. Whether or not Fergus indulged in such imaginings Flora had no way of knowing. But she doubted if his mind was haunted, as was hers, by the presence of that little scrap of humanity; after all, in a strictly clinical sense their daughter had never lived at all.

Nowadays, or so Flora was led to understand, such things were managed differently. A mother was encouraged to look upon her stillborn child so that she might come to terms with, if not always accept, the finality of death, the shattering of expectation. All that memory afforded Flora was the recall of a terrible silence which had succeeded exhausted exhilaration. Then had come the whispering; the discreet laying aside; the grave faces looking down upon her from a seeming great distance. Later, and perhaps almost as difficult to bear, had come the brief assurances that, as she was young, there was lots of time ahead of her in which to bring forth another, and a living, child. 'It's not the end of the world, old girl!' Fergus had said, plonking a bunch of blood-red roses on the bed. No, perhaps it hadn't been; but it had felt very like it. He had gone on to open a bottle of champagne, 'to cheer us up' as he had put it – but Flora had suspected that it was really in order that it should not be wasted.

That pregnancy, Flora's first and, as it transpired, her last, had occurred shortly after Fergus's demobilisation at the end of the war. It had, as Fergus had said, put the kibosh on his plans to return to university to complete his law studies. A job must now be found and a home provided for Flora and his coming son, he had said. At the time it had seemed sensible. It had also seemed fortunate that Reggie Lomas, a friend met in the Army, had been trying to persuade Fergus to abandon his plans for entering his father's law practice and, instead, to join the depleted staff of the boys' preparatory school which he owned in Derbyshire.

Fergus's parents had not tried to dissuade him. Flora could not help thinking that it would have been kinder if they had tried, just a little, for form's sake if for no other reason. His mother, in fact, had said nothing at all. But Mrs Sinclair had frequently demonstrated her ability to convey her opinion without having to resort to the use of words.

His parents, Fergus and herself, had been in the drawing room of Laggan Lodge when Fergus had broached the subject of his plans for the future and the reason for their reformulation, his voice a little too loud, his stance – his forearm resting on the mantelshelf – too consciously nonchalant. Oh, that drawing room! The memory of it was still capable of casting a chill over Flora. She could visualise it now: its glossy white paintwork; the ice-blue damask that upholstered the sofas and chairs and hung bleakly at the long windows; the black-framed etchings with their expanse of white mounts; the grey carpet and the pale ivory figurines precisely arranged in the display cabinet behind glass that reflected the pale green leaves and silvered bark of the birch on the lawn beyond the terrace. The delphiniums that filled the tall Chinese vase on its pedestal between the east-facing windows had certainly not been artificial, so it must be a trick of memory that they had stood there in every season, those stiff spires with their close-packed papery flowers, so coldly immaculate.

Mrs Sinclair, her back to the room, had appeared to be engrossed in making some finicky readjustment to the spikes of flowers, but suddenly she had pivoted round on her high-heeled court shoes to face Fergus and Flora. The faint raising of her thin eyebrows, the brief dusting of one pale hand against the other conveyed, without benefit of words, 'You've made, and indeed gambolled upon, your bed and now you must lie upon it – however disordered it may be.'

Mrs Sinclair had never been at pains to disguise her disapproval of wartime marriages and that of her son in particular. She had made even less effort to conceal her opinion that Flora was not at all the type of daughter-in-law for which she had hoped. But she had been gracious enough to make it clear to Flora that it was her back-ground which rendered her so unsuitable for that role and that her disapproval of the match was not directed against Flora in any personal sense – well, not entirely. And indeed it was true that Mrs Sinclair had rarely felt obliged to give much consideration to Flora as a person, so she could reasonably be exonerated of prejudice on that score. Even the daughter of a small-town chemist must surely possess sufficient nous to appreciate such niceties of social prejudice. But, as she had crossly pointed out to Flora on learning that a grandchild was on the way, Flora – working as she so regrettably did in her father's shop – might at least have been relied upon not to have incurred an unplanned and inopportune pregnancy. Flora, embarrassed, had felt unable to explain that she had access only to the account books and not to the secrets of the cupboard at the back of the shop which contained 'requisites' of whose purpose her father believed a nice girl should be in total ignorance.

In the event, as Flora remembered it, Fergus had not seemed too cast down by the change in his plans. One could have gained the impression that he was relieved that he would not be returning to university, had it not been for the fact that he frequently reminded her, and anybody else who happened to be listening, of his sacrifice of that prospect. But, at the time, Fergus had said that the job at Windy Ridge would do very well – pro tem, naturally.

I ought to go back to the house, Flora told herself, glancing at her watch. Fergus liked his lunch to be served on time. Perhaps it was a lifetime ruled by bells and timetables that had made him so obsessive about routine, Flora told herself, preferring not to consider that Fergus feared that without routine the structure of his existence would disintegrate entirely. But before I go, she decided as she pushed herself up from the chair, I may as well water the plants.

There was one thing to be said in favour of the dying of the year, she consoled herself as water gushed from the verdigrised tap, splashing into the watering can and over her feet, and that is that the garden chores will begin to ease off. It was not that Flora disliked gardening; in fact she was rather fond of it, but in moderation.

They've done well, she congratulated herself, admiring the broad-hipped peppers hanging scarlet as sealing wax among their dark leaves. The tomato plants were practically leafless, but that circumstance did expose the few remaining trusses of under-sized fruit to the full benefit of such sunlight as penetrated the algae-stained glass.

A sparrow found its way in through a broken pane in the roof and crashed against the glass. Flora, anxious not to increase its panic, abandoned the watering can and walked quietly out, leaving the door propped open behind her. The birds found their way in with such ease, she thought, but getting out was another matter. More than once she'd discovered a bird, dead, huddled close against the imprisoning glass, its outstretched wings as stiff as parchment fans. She walked quickly away, unable to watch the frantic hither and thither flight, but the sound of the dull thuds made by the small body as it dashed itself again and again into the panes pursued her, even beyond earshot.

The dense and dusty appearance of the shrubbery dividing the kitchen garden from the back lawn was enlivened only by the glimmer of the white trumpet flowers of the convolvulus which clambered, unchecked, over the dark leaves of lilac and laurel. Below the rhododendrons, thrusting above the end-of-summer detritus, flamed the berried rods of cuckoo-pint but, despite such evidence that Spring was long past, here and there an occasional primrose or a violet also bloomed, perverse in their refusal to acknowledge that Autumn had arrived.

On the other side of the boundary hedge and just visible above it, something moved, disappeared briefly from sight and then rose again, wildly waving. Flora narrowed her eyes and brought into focus two feet, unshod but brightly clad in canary yellow socks.

Opening the back door, Flora could hear, from the kitchen, the voices of Eleanor and Letty. She hesitated, debating whether she could quietly make her exit, but Fergus had heard the opening of the door and bellowed, 'Thought you'd got lost!'

'Damn!' Flora muttered, unlacing her gardening shoes. And why does he take them into the kitchen? Surely only the most intimate of friends should be admitted to one's kitchen – my kitchen. Thank God they'd at least stopped bringing their slobbering old spaniel with them – lifting his leg when he thought you weren't looking and leaving his fleas behind. All very well for Fergus to insist that that was her imagination; Flora just knew that beastly Boots had fleas, he was forever scratching, except when he was trying to thrust his nose up her skirt.

14

Probably caught them from the donkey, Nicholas Nye. Nicholas Nye, indeed!

'Hurry up! Bring a glass with you if you want a snifter.' Fergus was using his gay-dog voice.

'Just coming!' And I won't be bringing a glass with me. Not, thought Flora, that my sitting there pointedly *not* having a drink ever seems to embarrass them in the slightest. Besides, anything other than a glass of sherry before lunch seemed rather dissolute.

The gin bottle was in the centre of the kitchen table. Fergus was by inclination a whisky man and had only started to stock gin when Eleanor had made it clear that that was her favoured tipple.

She was already well away, Eleanor, waving her glass around and gushing nonsense eighteen to the dozen. She must have been well tanked-up before her arrival, Flora decided, glancing quickly at the level in the bottle. It wasn't fair that despite her alcoholic intake Eleanor should remain so slim and attractive – for her age, Flora amended, confident in the knowledge that Eleanor was oblivious of her critical stare, having spared her only the briefest of glances since she had sat down. Eleanor's hair, Flora assured herself, was obviously touched-up. No woman in her sixties, early sixties or not, could still boast hair that was naturally ash-blonde. But the tinting was discreetly done, nothing brassy about the result; the colour complemented a faded complexion rather cleverly, one had to admit that. I wonder if Letty does it for her?

She has the type of face that I would call horsey, thought Flora, those fine and lightly fleshed bones and the large eyes . . . Fergus said that Eleanor had a 'well-bred' face. But then the odious and flea-infested Boots was also impeccably bred, an aged scion of a distinguished line of gun dogs – but he was obnoxious for all that!

'What have you been up to all morning?' Fergus was sloshing more gin into the glass which Eleanor had thrust towards him.

'Oh – things. Watering the tomatoes and so forth. None ready for picking though, they're more or less fin-ished for the season.' Flora added that information for Eleanor's benefit. She and Letty had first called on the pretext that they had always bought their tomatoes and lettuce from the dear old Wing-Co.

'I think it's too wonderful, all the things you manage to grow. I was just saying to Letty, the other day, that it quite puts us to shame! But then one either has green fingers or one hasn't.'

Letty said nothing, only smiled in her maddeningly enigmatic way, her full lips curving faintly upwards, her little square teeth concealed. It was a smile that seemed to say, 'The things I could tell you . . . if only I chose to!' And I bet she could too, thought Flora. How can she stand it, being general dogsbody and companion to Eleanor – and probably unpaid. But perhaps she is paid by Alastair, whose name cropped up occasionally in the course of conversation as Eleanor's husband, divorced or separated was never made clear; it could be that he employed her to keep an eye on Eleanor. On the other hand, I wouldn't put it past Letty to accept payment from both of them; she would if she could. One gathered that she was some sort of relation, but whether the relationship was with Eleanor or Alastair was also unclear. But she was certainly out of the same drawer and, considering the inbreeding that went on with that class of person, Letty might well be related to both. But what a way to live! I'd rather starve, thought Flora. But that alternative would be unthinkable for roly-poly Letty.

Eleanor, her glass topped up, had turned her attention back to Fergus.

'But you *must* have known the Menzies at Tomnatain? She was a Carmichael before she married Donald, a bit loopy, actually, but great fun!'

'I know who you mean, of course,' Fergus hastily assured her. 'I seem to remember fishing there with my father back in—'

'Well, anyway,' Eleanor broke in impatiently, irritated that some people seemed unable to distinguish which questions really demanded an answer and which were interposed merely to give the listener the impression that he was taking part in a conversation, 'Alastair and I were there for the shooting that October and . . .'

Here we go, thought Flora, making a conscious effort to block out Eleanor's voice with her own thoughts and wishing that she had taken a drink after all. They're playing their favourite game, Scots in exile; upper-crust Scots, naturally. Gracious! One would think that they were expatriates in some far-flung outpost of what had been the Empire, instead of sitting quite comfortably in Sussex. And as for Fergus! There he sat all ready to turn dewy eyed or to laugh uproariously as might be required. Who did he think he was fooling – apart from himself? Even Eleanor must be well aware that Fergus had never moved in her circles. Fergus's father might have been regarded as moving on the periphery, so to speak, of the county set but only in so far as that he was occasionally invited by some of his more aristocratic clients to enjoy a day's salmon fishing or shooting or even to be a weekend guest; but only towards the close of a poor season. Clients who had been in arrears in their payment for his professional services had been known to be quite generous in extending such patronage. Much as such little excursions had gratified the social aspirations of his wife, Mr Sinclair himself would never have claimed membership of that privileged Highland élite. Indeed he might well have found such a suggestion mildly insulting.

Letty had pulled Fergus's *Telegraph* towards her and, pencil stump poised, was pondering the crossword. Flora knew from experience how annoyed Fergus became if anyone ventured to fill in as much as one clue in his crossword, so it was a measure of his attention to Eleanor that Letty's action passed unobstructed.

'I don't think you want more, dear,' Letty murmured,

not lifting her eyes from the paper, as Eleanor reached out for the bottle.

To give Letty her due, thought Flora, as Eleanor's hand withdrew, she does seem to be able to exercise some control over her. Letty knows precisely when the time is ripe to get Eleanor on her feet and on her way while that manoeuvre is still physically possible and Eleanor has reached, but not gone beyond, the stage of being amenable to suggestion. Flora recalled with disgust the morning when Eleanor had arrived unaccompanied (Letty being up in London for the day) and had ended up, dead to the world, stretched out on the sofa. There she had remained until retrieved by an unflustered Letty in the early evening.

Eleanor's voice had ceased and Flora seized her chance.

'Mr Hazel is standing on his head again! In his garden.'

Two pairs of eyes turned towards her, Letty's were still on the crossword. Their regard held irritation, not interest.

'He's wearing bright yellow socks!'

'Yellow socks, eh? Well, he would. Frightful fellow. What gets me is that we're soaked by the taxman to pay his inflation-proof pension. Bloody civil servants!'

Flora, although she knew it was pointless, was about to expostulate that Fergus's conviction about Mr Hazel's previous occupation and present financial security was purely speculative, when Eleanor resumed her monologue.

'Well, as I was saying, Roddie opened the bedroom door and there, my dear, was this damned great heifer eating the curtains!'

When Fergus had finished laughing (how does he manage it? Flora wondered with grudging admiration, having heard – or at least half-heard – the story on at least three previous occasions), he leaned forward and, his tone confidential, said, 'Do you know, rather a weird thing happened this morning. A bit sinister really.' Fergus paused, took the pack of cigarettes from his pocket and slapped it down on the table.

Before he could say more, Letty's plump mottled hand shot out. She grabbed the pack and swiftly popped it into her bag.

'So they came! Such a nuisance having to give different names and addresses every time I send off the coupons. But they have this tiresome "one pack per household" rule and I expect that they can check addresses on a computer nowadays.'

'Do shut up Letty! Come on Fergus, I'm all agog!'

'Ah well . . . extraordinary thing but it's gone clean out of my head. My memory these days is something shocking. Flora—' Fergus turned towards her, flustered, 'In case I forget – Eleanor's invited us to dinner, Friday evening.'

'How nice!' Flora emulated Letty's secretive smile all the more successfully for having glimpsed a trace of entreaty, or possibly panic, in Fergus's eye.

'Right then, that's all settled. Expect you quarter-to for

eight.' Letty had hitched the strap of her bag higher on her shoulder and, one hand firmly under Eleanor's arm, urged her to her feet. 'Come on, old thing!'

'Fergus, really! Why did you let them pin us down for dinner on Friday, surely you could have dodged it?'

Fergus was morosely prodding the herb omelette on his plate.

'I saw chops in the fridge.'

'And chops it would have been if that pair hadn't hung around for so long! I mean, it's half past two now and I know you planned to play a round this afternoon.' While I get the bean sticks down, thought Flora, slamming a bowl of watercress in front of him. A tiny creature like a minuscule lobster waved its legs in frantic protest before it and its supporting leaf disappeared below Fergus's moustache. Oh well, what the eye doth not see, thought Flora.

'I'm scrubbing golf this afternoon. Besides, we can't go on turning down Eleanor's invitations. Bad manners. She feels under an obligation – always accepting our hospitality but not being given the chance to reciprocate.'

'Oh rubbish Fergus! They don't *have* to keep coming here, do they? Certainly I've never invited them. In any case, they only come for the drink. If I'd known that we would have the feminine version of a remittance man only ten minutes from our door, then I'd never have agreed to move here!'

Not that I was given an opportunity to agree or to disagree, Flora reminded herself, and that grievance still rankled. Oh she'd guessed that there had been something in the wind; that Fergus had been turning over plans of action in his mind. But that Fergus would actually do something – anything – and so swiftly and irreversibly, that had been quite unforeseen. Not for a moment had she thought that Fergus had been about to abandon a lifetime's policy of refraining from positive action. She'd sensed no danger even when Fergus had said that he would seize the opportunity presented by the half-term break to visit the south and look at a few houses. Make a recce, he had said. The discovery, on his return, that everything was settled, cut and dried, and that they were to move to Sussex, had come as a great shock. But that Fergus had at last cast off the painter only in order that they might sail, prematurely, into quiet harbour, had not been so surprising. Everything, Flora thought, could be attributed to a fortuitous combination of circumstances.

'Wasn't there a letter from Stella this morning?' she asked, suddenly remembering.

Fergus was making heavy weather of peeling a Laxton. Well, if he would insist on the windfalls being used, then that was his look out. Such petty economies were perhaps necessary if one was to keep a stock of gin in the sideboard!

'That's right, there was. Not so much a letter as a brief note dashed off, no doubt, on her way to or from some high-powered business conference! She deigns to pay us a visit this weekend before she goes to Switzerland – she's flying from Gatwick, so it probably suits her to leave from here. See for yourself.' Fergus fished in his pocket and tossed his sister's letter to Flora before turning his attention back to his plate.

'God! There's some sort of maggot in this apple!'

'Not a maggot, dear,' Flora corrected him absent-mindedly, her eyes already eagerly on the letter, 'a caterpillar, most likely a codlin moth. The apple trees are absolutely infested, they should have been sprayed. I did tell you.'

She folded the letter carefully and placed it in her cardigan pocket.

'Well, that's splendid! She'll be arriving some time on Saturday morning and needn't leave until Monday.'

'I know, I know – I did read it!' Fergus was mopping his moustache, pushing back his chair. 'Must be off!'

'But I thought you said that you weren't playing golf after all?'

'Promised to pop over to Eleanor's. Couple of planks have worked loose on that shelter I knocked up for Nicholas Nye.'

'To hell with the bean sticks!' Flora proclaimed to the silent kitchen, to the stacked dishes in the sink, the saucer of bloodworms thawing on the draining board in readiness for the fishes' evening feed.

23

A walk was the answer. She'd take the car and drive to where she could walk beyond sight of Hillcrest, its garden and the too-close town.

We no longer have need of a car this size, she told herself, backing the decrepid shooting-brake down the short drive, edging it cautiously between the crumbling gateposts. It had had its day: ferrying small boys down the narrow stone-dyked roads of Derbyshire to dental appointments in the town, taking them on shopping expeditions, visits to the opticians, but now . . . she'd tackle Fergus about it. Yet again.

Flora headed for the main road. The lane was a cul-de-sac which ended at the entrance to the neglected Grange where Eleanor and Letty lived out their left-over days. Mr Hazel's gimcrack bungalow almost nudged Hillcrest, having been built in a part of Hillcrest's grounds annexed for that purpose in the thirties. Sad, lean ponies grazed the starved meadowland that bordered the lane. On one corner of the junction with the road stood the square brick house where the Protheroes lived.

Flora, waiting for a break in the traffic, glanced at the Protheroes' garden. It was untidy, but it was the untidiness of usage rather than weary neglect. A caravan was parked just off the drive and Mrs Protheroe in ink-blue jeans was cleaning its windows. She smiled and briefly waved a chamois leather in the direction of Flora. Two small children in dungarees tacked round the end of the house carrying a bucket of water between them. Perhaps,

24

thought Flora, it's as well that I am only on smiling and waving terms with the Protheroes. Closer acquaintance might reveal that they weren't as happy and contented a family as she liked, indeed needed, to imagine them to be. But the superficial acquaintance was unlikely to develop into a more intimate relationship; after all, Flora was old enough to be Mrs Protheroe's mother. Her own daughter might, by now, have been just such a one as Mrs Protheroe, and her children, Flora's grandchildren. Flora snatched at the wheel, turning the car tightly left.

She parked at a field entrance and strode energetically along the footpath, heedless of the cows that suspended their ruminative chewing to stare after this short and sturdy woman who marched across their territory with such profligate energy, her soft thick hair gleaming silver in the afternoon sun.

Not until she tackled the rising ground did Flora begin to slacken her pace. Close to the top of the hill, a straggle of wind-skewed broom at her back, she sat down. The Downs seemed to shift and stir around her as the shadows of the clouds skittered across the sun-bleached grass.

Flora closed her eyes for a moment and allowed the scent of the broom, sweet and light in the last of the summer's warmth, to evoke vague, half-formulated memories. Somewhere a sheep bleated, a lost, plaintive sound.

She blew her nose, dabbed at her eyes and told herself

that it was only the pollen from the grass and the breeze, quite sharp up here on the shoulder of the hill, that had made them run with tears.

Here, she thought, with the sprawl of the town hidden from sight, one was in a different world. How she resented the proximity of the town.

'A charming market town' was how Hopkins had described it in his suave estate agent tone of voice. Fifty years ago, or perhaps only twenty, charming it might have been. But no longer could it be so described. Its heart had been torn out to make room for what was described as 'a modern shopping precinct'. High-rise office blocks, aglint with glass and steel, rose incongruously above what remained of the narrow homely streets, dwarfing even the steeple of the ancient parish church as though bearing witness to the supremacy of a new god. From the upstairs windows of Hillcrest one looked down upon an industrial estate and the warren of a new housing development that bit into the fields beyond the disused branch railway track which ran, like a rusty-red boundary line, at the foot of the steep hill upon whose summit Hillcrest perched. Flora found herself in agreement with what had been her Aunt Agnes's dictum – one should live either in a city or in the country because that which was neither the one nor the other was to be abhorred. 'God made the country', Aunt Agnes had been prone to quote, 'man made the town, but the devil made the country town!'

Flora smiled a little, hearing again her aunt's voice, sometimes acerbic but always confident. Oh, to have inherited a little of her certainty, her decisiveness of action, her dogged determination! But perhaps Agnes had not really been like that . . . or, at least, not only that. After all, when I remember her, remember any of them, I can see them only through the eyes and with the perception of the child that I then was.

It had been women, Flora acknowledged, who had dominated the days of her remembered childhood. Uncles, both paternal and maternal, had been winnowed away by the Great War. Only the maiden aunts had survived, Agnes and Annie. There had also been Mother and her paternal grandmother. Father too, of course, but her memory of him was shadowy, elusive; it was only his physical presence which she could bring vividly to mind: Father, dapper in his striped trousers and black jacket, his small neat shoes almost hidden below his dove-grey spats. His lapel had almost invariably displayed a buttonhole, a flower freshly plucked each morning by Flora's mother. But however sweet the scent of the buttonhole, it was always overlaid by the distinctive aroma of medicaments that clung to its wearer – the aroma of the dispensary and the chemist's shop.

Is it a self-indulgent vice, Flora asked herself, something I should at least try to control, this growing habit of recollection? I scoop up times past as though they were so many pebbles to be held in my hand, selecting one for closer examination, discarding another, arranging them this way and that in the hope that a pattern may emerge. Do I persist in the hope that one day sense and order will emerge instead of random confusion and that I will see some purpose in what has been and, by definition, in what has yet to come? Or perhaps I only delude myself in ascribing any logical reason for my new-found obsession with the past.

Aunt Annie would have dismissed the activity as being no more than 'wool-gathering'. Aunt Annie had been in a position to recognise in others the propensity for wool-gathering, she herself having been prone to indulge in that pursuit. In a quite literal sense too, thought Flora, smiling to herself as she permitted her memory a contin-ued freedom. Annie had hoarded wool. An old pillowslip had bulged with her collection: scraps left over from her knitting of garments, whole skeins bought cheaply from remnant bins, bullet-hard balls of wool which had been unravelled from old garments and then tightly wound in a brave attempt to straighten out the crinkles.

Sometimes, when visiting her grandmother and Annie, Flora would be invited to tidy the wool bag. Aunt Annie would extend the invitation as though proffering a special treat and, perhaps as a result, Flora had quite enjoyed the task. Sitting quietly in some corner of her grandmother's cluttered and stuffy sitting room, patiently unravelling the multicoloured yarns, her silent presence was soon for-gotten and the conversation of the adults would flow over her head – but not always above her understanding. Occasionally Aunt Agnes would also be present, but not very often, the train fare from Edinburgh to the Highlands putting some strain on the modest budget of a nursing sister.

There had been little common ground of agreement between Flora's grandmother and her two spinster daughters, but there had been two topics of discussion in which they had found themselves in complete rapport with one another. The first was their mutual resentment of the circumstance that, on his marriage, Flora's father had installed his wife in the family home and his mother and sister Annie had had, as a consequence, to remove themselves to the cramped little Victorian villa in Abernethy Close. Fortunately – or not, according to how one regarded the result – old Mr Munro's will, while stating quite categorically that his surviving son should inherit the business and, on marriage, the house, had not specified in any detail which of the house's contents might be removed to Mr Munro's other property – the villa in which his widow and dutifully attendant daughter now found themselves. Flora's grandmother had, predictably, crammed into her second home as much as was possible of the furniture of Larchdale. Indeed, she had managed to accommodate more articles than one might have considered possible, and certainly more than most would consider desirable. Crags of dark mahogany loomed against the walls of every room – chiffoniers, sideboards,

monstrous wardrobes of imposing proportions. In the sitting room, one's progress across the floor was impeded by
a wealth of small tables, several pouffes and a clumsy can-
terbury. But still Mrs Munro bewailed the loss of a
particular chair, grieved over the absence of a favourite
ewer, felt robbed of the comfort of a particular hearth
rug. Despite her declared ambition to sit at the right
hand of God, Grandmother had shown no reluctance to
lay up for herself treasures upon earth. Annie, for her
part, rarely set the tea-table without remarking that her
jam never reached the same perfection of set and colour
as it had before she had been dispossessed of the copper
preserving pan which, by some oversight, had remained
in her sister-in-law's rapacious grasp.

That had been their second topic of harmonious discussion: the shortcomings of Flora's mother. Flora could
not remember a time when she had been unaware that
her grandmother had little regard for her daughter-in-
law. According to old Mrs Munro, Nelly (Flora's mother)
had been no more than 'a scheming shop-girl with an eye
to the main chance'.

In age, Mrs Munro had developed the disconcerting
habit of uttering such pronouncements regardless of the
subject matter under discussion. Her statements, frequently startling, were voiced in a musing tone which led
the bewildered listener to assume, rightly or wrongly,
that the old woman was unaware that her aberrant
thoughts were being given utterance. In this way, Flora

learned many things of which she would otherwise have been in ignorance.

Not all of her grandmother's statements had been verifiable; which had been, perhaps, just as well. One afternoon, while the minister's wife was being entertained with tea and scones, Mrs Munro had, without preamble, dropped into a pause in the conversation the words: 'Cousin Sheila finished her off, y'know. Put something in her Ovaltine. Fancy that now, my aunt murdered by her own daughter!' She had given a little giggle, surprisingly impish for one of her years and dour disposition, as she smeared a dollop of jam on her scone. Aunt Annie had flushed, vigorously shaken her head and frantically mouthed a denial of this intriguing information. The minister's wife, doubtless accustomed in the course of her parish visiting to hearing such senile wanderings, had been the first to regain her gracious equilibrium. But Flora had remained open-mouthed for some seconds, indeed until brought to heel by a sharp rebuke from her grandmother: 'Catching flies are you, child?'

'The child', they were fond of referring to me as that, perhaps because I was the only example of the species under their immediate scrutiny, thought Flora. It was only as she had started to grow beyond the very early years of childhood that she had realised that there were disadvantages to being the focus of so much attention. When small, she had intuitively exploited her situation of being between two rival factions. She had sensed that her grandmother and the aunts were eager to pull her into their camp while her mother, on the other hand, jealously exercised her rights of possession, her pride of ownership being rather more apparent than any feelings of deep affection for her daughter.

But, once such a consideration became appropriate, all of them - Grandmother, the aunts and Mother – had shared a preoccupation in common; and that was that Flora should be made aware of the importance of retaining her virginity. Not, of course, that any one of them had expressed that intention with such clarity.

When, at thirteen, Flora had (to her own embarrassment and alarm) produced irrefutable evidence of having embarked upon puberty, her mother had, in solemn tone, informed her: 'This means that one day you will grow up into a woman'. Had Flora been harbouring delusions that she might mature into a giraffe or an elephant, that intelligence might have served some practical purpose but, as it was, Flora found it singularly uninformative. Her mother had added, enigmatically, 'Never forget that her purity is a young woman's most valuable possession.' Her mother had, unaccountably, seemed full of a self-important pride and had confided to Flora that she was glad that 'it' had not happened any earlier as it was not considered nice for girls to be too precocious in that respect. Some days later, her face averted, her hands busily occupied in a mixing bowl, Mrs Munro had haltingly imposed some further advice upon her mystified daughter.

A woman, she had said, must never let a man have what he wanted – unless she was married to him, in which case, of course, she had no option. But if an unmarried girl allowed a man to have his way, to jump the gun, then he would never lead her to the altar; and what sensible girl with her head screwed on right would want to risk being left on the shelf?

Aunt Annie's advice had been even more circumlocutory. No man in his senses, according to her, would be able to resist the charms of Flora's beautiful hair and her lovely figure. Meantime, until Mr Right came along, Flora should mind her P's and Q's and resist the blandishments of all the admirers the future would undoubtedly hold. 'Don't ever do anything that you felt you couldn't tell your old aunty about, child,' she had entreated, gazing moistly through her thick lenses upon her blushing niece.

Grandmother had said, darkly, that the Lord worked in mysterious ways and not the least mysterious were his arrangements for the continuance of the human race. A woman just had to accept that sort of thing, remember her Christian duty and go to her married bed pure in mind and body.

Aunt Agnes had been brusque. Men, she had said, were selfish and stupid creatures, intent upon snaring women into servitude and morbidly eager to deprive them of that which a woman should preserve intact. If men got from you what they lusted after, then you lost their respect. If you did hold out until, in desperation, they offered marriage, then that state would eventually deprive you of your own self-respect and rob you of all identity as a human being in your own right.

It had all been very puzzling. Her hair and her figure (developing a disturbing localised plumpness within the confines of her liberty bodice) were, apparently, to be Flora's lure; but what, exactly, was the trophy that had to be guarded so carefully and preserved intact until marriage permitted its bestowal?

The Home Doctor acted as a bookend to the novels of Ruby M. Ayres and *A Simple Guide to Stitchcraft* which stood on a shelf in her mother's bedroom. Flora's rather muddled and, of necessity, surreptitious study of that fat volume provided little enlightenment. But by a process of cross-reference she did come across the world 'maidenhead', which had an intriguing ring to it and evoked visions of scalps and shrunken heads.

To her own surprise, Flora found herself looking back with tenderness rather than exasperation to the innocence of her girlhood. She could even feel tolerantly amused rather than angered by the memory of the total inadequacy of the advice that had been proffered in preparation for life. No one, least of all herself, had questioned the assumption that marriage should constitute the ultimate goal for a woman.

The young today, she told herself a trifle defensively,

may be blasé know-alls but, for all their apparent competence, they don't seem to be able to live their lives with
any more success than their elders brought to that chal-
lenge. What, after all, could possibly prepare one for the
sheer random nature of life? Does anyone really understand how one ought to cope with life or even come to
terms with it – far less know how to live it successfully?

The light was beginning to wane, draining away from
the Downs like colour withdrawing from a weary face; the
dewpond no longer winked in the sunshine but sulked
darkly in its hollow. Rabbits were emerging, lulled into
boldness by her stillness.

Flora clambered to her feet, her movement scattering
the little homely nursery shapes. It was time to go
home – or, at least, time to return to Fergus and
Hillcrest.

2
~

At least he was asleep at long last, the quilt up to his ears and the blankets all yanked to his side of the bed. Flora gave a tentative pull at the sheet. Fergus groaned.

It must be quite three o'clock, she thought, staring into the stuffy darkness but not daring to switch on the light for fear of rousing Fergus. It had been half past two when she'd stumbled down to the kitchen to fetch him another couple of Alka-Seltzers, the first dose having been noisily regurgitated in the bathroom.

His sickness couldn't be due only to the drink, she thought, although goodness knows, he'd had more than enough of that. No, it must have been the chicken. The kipper pâté that had preceded it had been pretty foul, but the chicken had been *the end*. Well, she'd tried to warn him, catch his eye as she'd seen the red juice oozing under the carving knife as Letty had struggled to sever the legs. But what with the dim candlelight and Fergus's head being constantly inclined towards Eleanor, her warning glances had gone unnoticed or unheeded. Pity he hadn't been near enough to kick.

One could contract something really nasty from eating frozen chicken which had been imperfectly thawed – myxomatosis, was it? Perhaps not, but certainly something very disagreeable. Flora tried to console herself with the thought that Letty and Eleanor would also be affected, together with their beastly dog who had greedily golloped down all of her own portion which Flora had fed to him under the table. She shuddered a little both from cold and the remembrance of the dog's soft slobbering lips on her hand. But no, Eleanor would be unscathed as she'd scarcely touched a morsel of food, being too intent on swilling wine and laughing extravagantly at Fergus's boring old anecdotes. And Letty? Well, she'd eaten only the outside slices of the breast. Sly Letty. She had probably been well aware that she'd forgotten to take the damned bird out of the freezer in good time – Flora could just imagine her dunking its iron-hard nakedness in a bowl of hot water.

They'd never left the table the whole evening – just sat on and on with the empties piling up while Flora had grown increasingly aware of the dusty disorder lurking in the corners of the room beyond the light shed by the candles. Probably Eleanor had been afraid to risk standing up; but, be that as it may, thought Flora, she'd retained a certain air of . . . well, graciousness . . . damn it!

Fergus had looked distinguished, but then Fergus always did – or at least when he was on show. It was a pity that he was so aware of it. He wasn't fat, not yet, but there really was a lot of Fergus; really too much, she thought, trying once more without success to tug some of the bedclothes away from the great mound at her side.

I did try to get them to move away from the dining room and the all too accessible bottles, thought Flora, reminding herself of how she'd leapt up to assist Letty when she'd gone to make the coffee, hoping that she could carry the tray into the drawing room. Well, anything was preferable to being stuck like a supernumerary at the foot of the table with that disgusting smelly Boots resting his head on my lap and snuffling his expectation of more titbits. I mustn't forget to sponge and press my skirt.

She'd helped to clear some of the dishes too, carried them into the kitchen. Oh that kitchen! Letty had stopped her from putting the cream jug in the sink and had placed it instead in front of the cat who was sitting on the draining board intent on indelicate ablutions. After Letty had thrown the chicken bones on the boiler fire, she had then placed the dinner plates in a row on the floor for the dog's attention.

Well, all in all it serves Fergus right that he's sick. I don't feel the least bit sorry for him, she told herself, edging a little further away from his now snoring bulk.

I'd slip into the spare room if it wasn't for the bed being freshly made up in readiness for Stella's arrival tomorrow; no, it's today now. And that's another thing, thought Flora, giving the quilt a reckless and vicious pull, he *would* knock himself up just when Stella is coming. But that might not be altogether a bad thing, she reflected, the retrieved quilt restoring her circulation. With him safely out of the way in bed, Stella's visit might pass without a flaming row developing. That would make a change!

How strange that last glimpse of Eleanor had been. Flora had looked round before reaching the curve in the drive which would hide the house from view and had waved to Letty who was standing at the open door. Suddenly, there was Eleanor in her long grey lace, yawing across the lawn at the side of the house, like a wraith in the moonlight. She'd urged Fergus to look. 'She'll be going to say goodnight to Nicholas Nye; always does. She really loves that animal,' Fergus had said, as though the bizarre sight was the most natural thing in the world.

Flora, drifting eventually towards sleep, thought with a touch of envy about poor Nicholas Nye – certainly old, grey and lame of a leg but, like his namesake, 'asking not wherefore nor why'.

Fergus must be feeling really rocky to have entrusted me with this little job, Flora thought, sprinkling the carefully measured morning feed into the aquarium.

They really are very beautiful, she conceded. Electric blue and orange and black damsels, pinky-gold antheas with lemon-coloured fins, and multi-coloured harlequins weaved gracefully in and out through the fronds of the marine plants. A clown fish tumbled through the water, curtseying and dipping, the white bands on its ochre body so precise that they might have been painted on; indeed she noticed that the bands were thinly black-edged as though a draughtsman's pen had defined their exact placing.

Out of their caves in the coral slid Fergus's particular favourites, the pair of wafer-thin butterfly fish. Insubstantial as sheets of shimmering gold leaf they swam upwards, towards her hand, hesitated uneasily, their preposterous long black noses just breaking the surface of the water. Suddenly they were gone, falling like leaves to the bottom of the tank, insinuating themselves horizontally into the mouths of their coral caves.

I wonder, thought Flora as she waited patiently, a scrap of bloodworm dangling from her poised fingers . . . I wonder . . . Slowly, his inquisitiveness overcoming caution, one of the butterfly fish glided out from hiding and up through the water he swam again. Flora held her breath. Swiftly the worm was snatched from her fingers, the snapping of the fish's jaws clear and sharp in the silence.

Flora felt unreasonably elated, as though a special honour had been bestowed. But I won't tell Fergus, she decided; he'd never forgive me – or them. He had spent months training the butterflies to feed from his hand and would think it intolerable that they should prove to be so undiscriminating in the granting of their favour.

The food all gone, she dabbled her fingers briefly in the water, washing them . . . or waving a brief farewell? If I'm allowed to tend them again this evening, then I'll definitely call the doctor to have a look at Fergus, she told herself.

The fish, startled by the disturbance made by her fingers in the water, rushed excitedly around the tank and dived for the shelter of the corals where they remained, palpitating, their mouths working with apparent indignation. The little frog-faced mandarin, mosaic-patterned in burnt orange and blue and forever skulking on the sandy bottom for all the world like a scrap of glazed pottery, stared out at her, his popping swivel eyes still for once, just staring. He looked, all three inches of him, positively belligerent. What nonsense, Flora chided herself, putting her tongue out at him.

She gave the glass a little tap, sending them all whisking through the water in panic. Stupid, smug creatures, frittering their lives away just eating, drifting dozing, posing! The mandarin moved not a fraction; he just stared.

Fergus was bawling something from upstairs. Can't be all that ill if he can shout like that, Flora thought, going out into the hall.

41

'Have you checked the temperature?' he yelled again, a querulous note in his voice now.

'Yes, dear. Eighty degrees. But precisely!'

'Hmmph. Any chance of some beef tea? I feel a bit empty.'

Beef tea, indeed! She remembered a tin of consommé on the larder shelf.

'I'll see what I can do. But it'll take about an hour to make y'know!' Keep him waiting and he might actually think it was the real thing. There were some advantages after all in Fergus not knowing even how to boil an egg.

Meantime, she decided, I'll do the flowers. She went into the garden to pluck them, the blooms still crisp and fresh in the morning air. How nice it must have been, she thought, plucking and choosing, sniffing and snipping, to have been one of those ladies of leisure whose only brush with gardening had been in choosing the flowers for their 'arrangements'. But perhaps leisure hadn't made them really happy – at least not if the example of Fergus's mother was anything to go by.

Flora wanted everything to be just right for Stella and there were three areas over which she had control: the flowers, the food and, of course, the attention to details of comfort in the spare bedroom. The interaction between Fergus and his sister was something that defied management and about which she would prefer not to think. One could always pray; the last refuge, she thought, whispering under her breath, as she gently parted a spray of rosebuds from their bush, the prayer that had been Aunt Annie's favourite: 'Trust the past to the mercy of God, the present to His love, the future to His providence.' God knows, thought Flora, I heard poor Annie murmur that often enough – well, if God hadn't known, then Annie had been cruelly deceived! Flora had seen a television film in which Svetlana Stalin and Malcolm Muggeridge had ambled across the Downs, tête à tête, and she remembered now how strange it had been to hear Svetlana quote the anodyne lines which had been of such comfort to Annie. But perhaps life in thrall to old Mrs Munro had not been so very dissimilar to life in the shadow of Stalin – it was simply a matter of degree.

Flora wrenched her mind back to the present and mentally checked her arrangements for Stella's visit. Stella, as Flora imagined her high-powered style of living, must be forever rushing here and there, staying in hotels, forced to eat ghastly things like prawn cocktails and Black Forest gâteau (caterers' style) or, alternatively, she would be eating scrambled eggs, solitary in her flat, or nibbling on a boring sandwich while still at her desk. But, tonight, Stella would dine off roasted leg of lamb, aromatic with garlic, marjoram and fresh rosemary and accompanied by the last of the mangetout and freshly cut spinach, beautifully creamed. There would be apple pie to follow, the first of the Bramleys spiked with quince and just dusted with ground cloves and cinnamon, the whole smothered in home-made custard. Real home cooking!

Flora was happy with the flowers, arranged in their containers on the kitchen table, waiting to be put in their respective places. There were marigolds in a willow pattern jug for the kitchen, late roses filled a crystal bowl to grace the dining table, and for Stella's bedroom there was a Victorian sugar basin filled with love-in-a-mist and gypsophila. Cape gooseberries and honesty, a portent of autumn, would suffice for the sitting room, the fish in their aquarium making any additional decoration almost superfluous.

Stella had been quite intrigued by the fish the last time she had come on a visit – well, her only visit until now. Of course Stella had an eye for colour, Flora reflected, giving the silver sugar basin an extra gentle buff with her handkerchief; an eye for colour, flair, these were surely some of the ingredients of her phenomenal success in the fashion world. 'Stella's Style' Who would have guessed that the rather grotty little shop that Stella had opened in the sixties to sell jeans and T-shirts would be the start of a chain of smart boutiques selling elegant, expensive clothes, mostly designed by Stella herself? She even had a foothold abroad. Yes, thought Flora, there was no doubt about it, Stella had got the measure of life, had control over her own; she knew how to change things, to adapt to circumstances and trends. Stella hadn't passively waited for opportunity to present itself but had forged it for herself. If only one could catch the trick from her – by a process of osmosis, as it were!

Flora was heating the consommé when Stella arrived. It was Stella who carried the soup up to Fergus. 'I'll play Hebe to his God,' she had said, whisking up the stairs. Flora, not wishing to go into details and also anxious that Stella should not fear infection, had ascribed Fergus's indisposition to a slight chill.

'You say it's a chill, but if you ask me, it looks remarkably like a hangover,' Stella had volunteered cheerfully on her return to the kitchen. 'And, do you know, he just stared at the label on the bottle of malt whisky I brought him, spotted the high proof, and said "Duty Free, I presume"!' But she was laughing, not offended – or, at least, not showing it.

Now that the bustle and initial excitement of her arrival were over, Flora felt slightly shy of this denizen from another world, standing there in her kitchen, so lively, so vibrant. But Stella is still young, only fifty-two or thereabouts, Flora told herself with the liberal view (which comes to us all with the advancing years) of what constitutes being past one's prime. But, even so, how, she wondered, does she manage to remain looking so positively youthful? Her slim figure and the quality of her clothes help, but there's more to it than that – it's also the lithe way she moves, her energy, confidence and . . . perhaps, a certain air of ruthlessness.

'Did you ask him if he felt like eating any lunch?'

'The soup's all he wants, apparently. He says he's going to stay where he is for the moment but he may feel like getting up by evening.'

'Good!' Flora did not clarify which part it was of that intelligence which pleased her. 'Let's have a little something out in the garden.'

'Lovely idea – just the two of us! Give me a tray and I'll help carry things out.'

Flora had already set up a little table in the lee of the shrubbery, sheltered from the wind. The chairs were strategically placed so that neither the unsightly greenhouse nor any of the more evidently neglected areas of the garden would meet Stella's gaze. The 'little something' was a fresh salmon mayonnaise – well, the fish had been frozen, but cooked with such care that Flora was confident that its inferior origins had been totally overcome, and certainly the watercress and avocado salad, the home-baked rolls and the lemon sorbet were beyond criticism. Next month's housekeeping money has been alarmingly broached, thought Flora, refilling Stella's glass with Chablis and regretting nothing.

'The garden's heavenly!' Stella's eye had been arrested by the glow and dazzle of the marigolds which Flora had planted in the vegetable garden to ward off carrot fly. 'I expect Fergus puts a lot of work into it. Good idea for him to have something to occupy his time, keep him busy.'

46

'He gets in quite a lot of golf. He likes that,' Flora answered cautiously, wondering if Stella was as guileless as her remark suggested.

'How do you feel about the move – d'you miss the school, Flora?'

'Yes, I do. I miss the boys and . . . oh, the general busyness, you know. Although I didn't have a specific job I was occupied with something all the time. I suppose I was a kind of Jack of all trades: helping with the paperwork, accounts, letters; giving Matron a hand when she needed it; doing the type of things a Head's wife would cope with, Reggie being unmarried then. You know the sort of thing, entertaining parents, dealing with visitors. Sometimes I used to take some of the younger boys for walks on the moors, sort of nature rambles. I liked that.' And there was never time to think, to question; perhaps that was the most important aspect of those years, Flora thought, with sudden insight.

'Still, you couldn't have had much opportunity just to be together on your own, you and Fergus. Not much time left for a private life in a boarding school, I imagine.'

'True.'

'Having a place of your own after all those years of living in a flat in the school, that must be terrific! Almost like being newly-weds all over again. You've made the house so nice, too,' Stella added, encouragingly, as Flora seemed disinclined to say anything. But, in truth, the furnishings of Hillcrest disturbed Stella, bringing her, as they did, in confrontation with the past; like a bizarre rerun of an old film, she thought. So much of the furniture had originally stood in Laggan Lodge.

To avoid arguments as to rights of possession (the argument being all of Fergus's making, as Stella remembered it), the furniture of Laggan Lodge had been auctioned after their mother's death and the proceeds added to the rest of the estate for equal division between brother and sister. Not that there had been much left to divide after Mrs Sinclair's creditors had been paid off. Fergus had attended the auction and now his purchases, their redolence of the past in no way diminished by their years in storage, occupied Hillcrest. Some things, Stella guessed, had come from Flora's old home The apothecary's marble mortar and pestle that stood on the kitchen dresser must once have belonged to Mr Munro, as had the elegant long-necked glass carboy which was now displayed on the landing window ledge. Stella remembered when it, or its twin, had stood in the window of the chemist's shop, filled then with a liquid of an improbable blue. In fact there was little that was new in Hillcrest; even the bed in the spare room Stella had recognised with startled dismay as having been the one in which her brother Bruce had slept as a child. These glasses on the table, they too had come from Laggan Lodge – was the rest of her mother's Edinburgh crystal ranged in the sideboard cupboard, heavy with remembrance of toasts long drunk and past? How could Flora bear it?

'I've never understood why you bought this particular place, I mean, it's so far from Derbyshire and the people you must know there.'

'Perhaps that's one of the things which decided Fergus to buy it.'

'But I thought that you both liked Derbyshire?'

'Yes, we did. But . . .' Flora hesitated, she didn't want to sound disloyal to Fergus but, after all, Stella did know what he was like. 'You see, I think he wanted to give everyone at the school the impression that he was retiring to something rather grand. "A little place in Sussex with a bit of ground and near a decent golf course" sounded rather good. And as it was quite a distance away there wasn't much danger of anyone actually looking us up. Besides, Fergus wanted to pretend that the move was something he'd been planning for some time. A free choice!'

'Wasn't it?'

'Not really. It was Reggie Lomas deciding to get married that changed everything. That announcement to the assembled staff – Fergus had not been told beforehand – well, it came like a bolt out of the blue! Fergus had got used to being Reggie's confidant so his nose had been properly put out of joint and, of course, he couldn't stand the prospective Mrs Lomas anyway. She was a widow, rather well-off and had plans for the school. She could afford to implement them too, with her sort of money. That was another thing, the money she could command made Fergus's modest investment seem very small beer indeed. Fergus suspected that changes wouldn't stop with her plans for building a science block and installing a new urinal in the changing rooms. There were sinister references to cutting out dead wood – and it was pretty obvious that she wasn't referring to the elms round the cricket field! Fergus could see himself being cast aside like an old boot – at least, that's how he put it.'

'Oh, how beastly for you Flora – well, for both of you. I'd no idea. Well, I had thought there must have been something; it didn't seem to me that Fergus could afford . . .' Stella broke off and added hastily, 'well, would *want* to retire. But why come to settle down here in this particular house – how did he even come to hear of it?'

'Oh, that was just one of those things. There was an Old Boys' Reunion just after Reggie'd dropped his bomb-shell and one of the men there . . .' Flora broke off to refill their glasses.

'God, how I disliked the O.B. affairs! The men who came were generally either the ones who'd been pretty disastrous as boys and then, if they'd made good, wanted to rub it in, to patronise the staff who'd failed to recog-nise their tycoon potential; and on the other hand there were the rather pathetic chaps whose schooldays had proved to have been literally the best years of their lives. They came back to wallow in memories of early tri-umphs, never subsequently matched. At least that's how it seemed to me – can't think what else they came for, couldn't have been for the claret cup and sausage rolls! It was the ones who'd turned out to be failures that Fergus used to like to talk to – telling them that material success was but a hollow thing . . . and all that rot!' Flora added tartly. 'Anyway,' she went on, 'how would he know about that – never having experienced it.' She paused. 'Where was I?'

'The Old Boys' Reunion,' Stella prompted.

'Yes. Well, at that particular reunion a chap called Hopkins turned up – in a Porsche, definitely one of the "see how well I've done" type! He'd become an estate agent – suited him, really. Apparently Fergus told him he was looking for a house for retirement and Hopkins suggested he looked at this place which was on the books of his Sussex branch and was going for a knock-down price subject to a quick sale. I'd always distrusted Hopkins as a boy – a sly, ginger-haired, plausible-tongued rogue. One could never actually pin anything on him although one just knew he was behind a lot of mischief. I nick-named him Macavity – after that cat, y'know!

'Anyway,' Flora lifted her voice in an attempt to make it sound as though what she had said was all of little consequence, 'that's how it was – and now you know!'

'I see. Well, perhaps he did you a good turn – it's a nice place, really.' Stella did her best to sound enthusiastic.

Flora said nothing, just shrugged.

'How are things . . . financially?'

Flora was grateful that the wine, the warmth of the sun, had already raised her colour so that her blush would pass unseen. Stella, she reminded herself, had always been direct and perhaps that, although it could be disconcerting, was really not such a bad thing.

'We manage.'

Stella leaned forward, the heavy gold chain round her neck swinging forward and gently tinkling against her plate. Meeting the gaze of her eyes, it struck Flora that that was one feature Fergus and Stella had in common, remarkably fine eyes of a deep, dark periwinkle blue. She wondered if Stella's, like those of Fergus, would fade with the passing years.

'Flora, don't let's be silly about this but, well, I'm not exactly short of a shekel or two; certainly more than I need even after the bloody taxman has had his clawback! So, if you're finding the going tough—' she waved a hand, impatient and dismissive of Flora's flustered attempt at interruption. 'Look, lots of people are up against it these days; inflation, all that. What I'm trying to say is that I'd be more than happy to help.'

'No!' She sounded so emphatic, that Flora startled herself. She added, quietly, 'Fergus would simply *hate* taking money from you – you must know that.'

Stella said nothing, drew back a little, lit a cigarette.

'Things are a bit tight, no good pretending they aren't,' Flora went on, embarrassed at the realisation that she might have been less than tactful. 'Frankly, I think it was a mistake to have moved here. For one thing, the garden's too much for me and paid help is out of the question. The rates are appalling. I hate the town and we don't seem to meet any people that I could take to – oh, you know what I mean! Something smaller, with a little, manageable garden, in a less expensive part of the country . . .'

'Have you spoken to Fergus about it?'

'Well, I've tried. But he doesn't want to be pinned down to a proper appraisal of hard facts. Plays hell when the bills come in but won't really *tackle* the problems. Just says we may as well stay where we are, pro tem.'

'I can just hear him saying that? "Pro tem." My God, that's the story of Fergus's life – "pro tem"!' Stella was laughing, her head thrown back, mouth wide open, showing a great deal of expensive bridgework.

Flora found herself laughing too. Suddenly nothing seemed so hopeless, so insoluble, not out here in the sunshine – Stella sitting opposite her, fresh and cheerful in her tailored blue linen; a young woodpecker calling jubilantly from somewhere among the apple trees.

Soon she was telling Stella about Eleanor and Letty, describing them as 'that poisonous pair'. She mimicked Eleanor's drawl, and the way she jerked one shoulder forward to pitch her breast into profile; she got up from the table and stumped, legs wide apart and arms akimbo in a parody of Letty's walk; she emulated Eleanor's babytalk as she fed apples to Nicholas Nye, even brayed his loving response.

53

Tears ran down Stella's cheeks and a peacock butterfly deserted the early Michaelmas daisies to sup delicately on the rim of a wine glass.

For two pins Flora would have stood on her head to demonstrate Mr Hazel's eccentricity. She kicked off her sandals, but, discretion coming tardily to her aid and a doubt arising as to her athletic capabilities, she threw herself instead into a deckchair and mopped her face, not caring about the damage she was wreaking upon her unaccustomed mascara.

'Do you know,' she gasped, 'I haven't felt so sane in months!'

3
~

Flora put the pastry for the apple pie into the refrigerator to rest. She had the kitchen to herself. Fergus was still in bed, Stella had gone upstairs to her room declaring that she had some paperwork to complete. Flora had taken a cup of tea to the recuperative Fergus and had quietly opened the door of Stella's bedroom with the intention of asking her if she too would like some tea. She had been comforted to discover that Stella was not quite the dynamo of energy that she had imagined her to be. Stella was stretched out on her bed, sound asleep, the contents of her suitcase untidily scattered around the room.

The vegetables have been brought in from the garden, thought Flora, ticking off items on her fingers, but the rosemary has still to be gathered.

The bush grew in a sheltered corner at the end of the back garden. From Mr Hazel's side of the hedge came a discreet murmuring of voices. Of course! Flora remembered that Mr Hazel was holding one of his 'gatherings' this afternoon. When he had first extended an invitation to Flora and Fergus to attend one of his 'gatherings', he had explained their function. 'A select group of worshippers of the Muse', as he had put it, mouthing the words with an air of gentle self-mockery, foregathered regularly at his home to listen to poetry readings and to refresh their spirits with discussion of the arts.

Mr Hazel's worshippers of culture, as Flora had observed when witnessing their arrival on previous occasions, were in the main female, and of a certain age. Two she recognised by sight, one of those being the lavender-haired Miss Cardew whom she was accustomed to see behind the counter at the building society. Their phatic exchanges over the prosaic transactions conducted there had given no indication to Flora that Miss Cardew harboured a reverence for the arts. The other woman, whose face was familiar but to whom Flora could not put a name, worked in the library and appeared to be the youngest of Mr Hazel's guests. The worshippers all bore with them, Flora observed as they filed up Mr Hazel's path, plastic boxes and covered plates which doubtless concealed the refreshments which Mr Hazel had told her (by way of added inducement) were always served. Flora had idly speculated about the nature of these offerings: confections of dates and honey, cream cakes and tiny cottage cheese sandwiches would be fitting she had decided, with no clear idea of the process of reasoning which had brought her to that assumption.

A voice, darkly rich and sonorous, floated over the hedge with awful resonance:

'Have you built your ship of death, O have you?
O build your ship of death, for you will need it.'

Flora, startled by this gratuitous injunction, wildly snatched a handful of rosemary and scuttled back to the kitchen, the voice pursuing her, the growing distance between herself and its source producing upon it a diminuendo effect which rendered the words more, rather than less, disturbing.

'The grim frost is at hand, when the apples will
    fall
Thick, almost thundrous on the hardened earth.
And death is on the air like a smell of ashes!'

Dear God, she thought, firmly closing the back door behind her – and to think that I was tempted to join Mr Hazel's group out of sheer desperation for a little social life to cheer me up!

The rosemary, crushed tightly in her hand, filled the kitchen with its scent, evocative of incense and sombre shadow. She switched the radio on, tumbled the basket of spinach into the sink and turned the tap full on in an effort to silence the words which echoed still in her head.

'I wonder that you haven't expanded in to the US of A.' There was a sarcastic edge to Fergus's voice.

'Oh, but that's definitely on the cards, Fergus. In fact I'm going to New York in the Spring to do a feasibility study.'

Well, that's definitely one up to Stella, thought Flora. Up to now the score had been running about even. It had been clear to Flora that Stella, out of compassion for Fergus's indisposition, had been generously conceding him the occasional triumph, had been pulling her punches. Fergus, on whom such subtleties were wasted, was becoming rasher, more offensive in his baiting.

'I think the boiled potatoes would be more digestible for you then the roasted, Fergus dear,' Flora suggested, hoping to remind Stella that Fergus was not quite up to scratch. It was really quite sad, she thought, to see him just pecking at the lamb when she knew that he loved it so.

'Do you know where I went last month?'

'I wouldn't dare hazard a guess,' said Fergus, helping himself to the largest and crispest roast potato in the dish.

Stella, ignoring the interruption, continued, 'I went back home. Strange to see the town again – after so many years. Full of ghosts. I stayed at the old Columba Hotel. Goodness, how it's changed!'

'Surely you're not thinking of opening a branch up there?'

'Why ever not, Fergus?' said Flora. 'I would have thought you'd like to think that a Sinclair was back in business there.'

'The Sinclairs were never in trade.'

'I can just see it!' Flora went on as though Fergus had not spoken. She sketched a signboard with her hands, '"Stella's Style" in Bridge Street, perhaps. The posh end, naturally; that should be a comfort to you, Fergus!'

'Huh!' said Fergus. 'I would have thought they've too much good sense up there to pay Stella's ridiculously inflated prices – even supposing they're daft enough to covet, what is it you call it . . . High Fashion?'

'You'd be surprised Fergus. Things do change you know. The women gave up shawls and pink flannel petticoats a few years ago now, even in the Highlands! And oil has poured a muckle of bawbees into the wee sporrans. But, I grant you, there are some things there that haven't changed all that much. The latest little storm in a teacup might amuse you!'

Fergus gave no indication of any potential to be amused.

'What's that then, Stella?' Flora asked obligingly, moving the spinach beyond Fergus's reach, it being, she considered, far too scouring for him in his present condition.

'Well, do you remember the Mackintoshs at The

59

Pines? You know, on Riverbank Road; oh, Fergus, you must remember them.'

'Accountant fellow, used to go curling with Father, wife built like a tank?'

'That's right. Well, of course, he's been dead for years and so is the odious Mrs M, although she hung on for years after him – have you noticed that that sort always do? But their daughter still lives at The Pines and—' Stella turned her sleek dark head towards Flora, '—Flora, you *must* remember her – Ishbel. The mousey girl who ran the Baby Linen, always looked as though she'd been frightened by something in the woodshed!'

Flora nodded, only dimly remembering but relieved that the conversation was taking what seemed to be a safe course. 'Do you remember' and 'Whatever happened to . . .' generally, in Flora's experience, ushered in chat of an innocuous, if not positively boring, character. There were occasions when it should be encouraged.

'Well, apparently Ishbel was left fairly well-off and she's used the money to turn The Pines into a pre-school playgroup. Filled the garden with climbing frames, swings and sandpits – you know the sort of thing. She has a couple of young Froebel teachers sharing the house with her as well as an old chap who collects the kids from town in a minibus. Of course, the other residents are up in arms, they're badgering the council to close it down. It ruins 'the tone' of the area, they say, and con-stitutes a change in usage of the property. Their real

60

gripe – although, naturally, they're not voicing it openly – is that most of the children are from one-parent families. Apparently Ishbel gives that category priority and reduced fees, takes them for nothing, in most cases, I believe. Encouragement of that sort of thing, and that sort of person, is beyond the pale in the eyes of her neighbours. One can almost hear old Mrs Macintosh thudding around in her grave!

'I must say, I take my hat off to old Ishbel! Who'd have thought she'd have the spunk? If she wants to put the money to good use and it makes her happy, then why should anyone have the right to stop her? My word, she earned every penny – looked after her dreadful mother for years, I gather. Sacrificed her life really – but not, as she is proving, quite *all* of it.'

'Mmm, must say I think the other residents have a point I'm sympathetic towards. I think that there's far too much trendy feather-bedding of the socially irresponsible; you've only got to look around you to see the mess that liberal permissive nonsense has got us into! But, that said, it certainly sounds as though this Ishbel woman did do her duty as far as her mother was concerned. Now, to *that* I take off *my* hat!'

Stella laughed. 'You never have forgiven me, Fergus, have you, for not sacrificing my life to the care of "dear Mother in her declining years" as you would probably put it!'

'Now I didn't say that Stella, but if the cap fits . . .'

61

'You may not have said it, but that's what you're getting at Fergus. All I can say is thank goodness I had the good sense to decide bugger that for a lark and clear out of Laggan Lodge!'

Fergus laid down his knife and fork with a clatter. 'I won't have that sort of language used at this table! I'll thank you to respect my wishes when you're under my roof. If you hadn't relinquished your duty in favour of your own frivolous and selfish pursuits then our dear mother's last years would have been very different.'

'Oh balls, Fergus! Mother had a very good time during her last years, at least by her peculiar standards. What you really mean is that if I hadn't insisted on living my own life, then Mother wouldn't have got into the hands of Nurse MacIver who pandered to her hypochondria and fleeced her very nicely in the process! All those fantastically expensive cruises; not to mention extra domestic staff to wait on the wily MacIver hand and foot. And who engaged MacIver? *You* did Fergus! I remember you saying what excellent references she had, nurse–companion to the Dowager Lady MacSporran, or some such tosh! Damned funny nurse she turned out to be – when after years of gadding about with that woman in attendance Mother did finally succumb to a stroke, the admirable MacIver popped her into a nursing home while she beetled off to open up a very profitable home "for gentlewomen" in Dunoon! But Mother had had a whale of a time and it was *her* money that she squandered – hard cheese on you, of course, that she spent what you'd hoped would eventually land in your lap.'

'How *dare* you . . .'

Flora ran from the room, hastily grabbed the apple pie from the oven and rushed it to the table.

'Apple pie, our very own Bramleys! I'm sure you could risk a tiny slice, dearest?' she turned to Fergus, smiling wildly, 'with a little custard.'

I might as well not be here at all, and how I wish I weren't, she thought, desperately sucking her knuckles where they'd brushed the side of the oven. Fergus stormed on, glaring at Stella and waving his dinner knife about in an alarming fashion. Stella was smiling in a rather supercilious fashion, but her eyes were very bright.

Fergus paused for breath.

'Do you know,' said Flora, plunging bravely in, 'I *do* remember Ishbel quite well, when I put my mind to it. But I seem to remember that there was another woman in that shop, a plump, dressy little body, rather jolly; now whatever was her name?'

'Oh that was randy Kirsty! There was more to her than two-ply and lavender sachets. Daddy had it off with her for years! Poor old devil, nice to think he had some comfort in life.'

Fergus has risen, his face so ashen that his moustache looked positively garish by contrast.

'Not another word!' he bellowed. 'That sort of filthy talk and innuendo may go down well with the company you keep – nancy boys and perverts! I wasn't born yes-terday, I know the kind of scum that infest your lounge-lizard world. "Rag Trade", a good name for it, if y'ask me: rags, an occupation for tinkers. To think that I'd live to see the day when my own sister . . .'

Fergus came to a spluttering halt, suddenly pulled himself up very straight and said with icy dignity, 'I'm going upstairs, away from this pollution.'

Flora had scrambled to her feet, her hand fluttered towards his sleeve.

Fergus drew away, 'I'm quite all right, thank you. I'll leave you *ladies* to your gossip.'

'But Fergus . . . look, I'm sure it's just Stella's fun.' She looked imploringly towards Stella who was calmly cutting herself a slice of apple pie. 'Sit down, do Fergus. I'll bring you something – a little brandy, perhaps?'

'No, no!' Fergus was already at the door, his napkin drooping incongruously from his trouser band like an unpinned nappy. 'I'll try to forget what you said, Stella, make allowances for your shortcomings – God knows, I've had enough practice! No, don't worry about me.'

'Goodnight, Eeyore,' Stella murmured, but Fergus was already plodding across the hall.

Flora sat down, her legs shaky, her mouth dry.

Stella refilled their glasses and then pushed back her chair.

'Let's go and sit by the fire – you've no idea what a treat an open fire is for me!'

Flora hesitated. The table in its disarray had, as yet, a not wholly unattractive appearance, presented, indeed, an illusion of conviviality. One could nurse the illusion that the barely broached apple pie would yet be eaten, the brie on the sideboard consumed to the crackle of biscuits and the noise of light, amiable chatter. Later, viewed with a cold and weary eye, it would be seen as a sordid mess, a memento of disaster, and the slop of wine beside Fergus's plate, untended, would have irretrievably stained the linen.

Seeing her hesitation, Stella said with an edge of exasperation, 'Oh for God's sake, Flora, leave it! We'll clear it up in no time after we've had our coffee. Come on.'

In front of the sitting-room fire, the two armchairs drawn companionably together and fresh logs singing and hissing as they settled between their glowing fellows, Flora felt she had achieved, if nothing else, a small triumph over her slavish, housewifely instincts, but a nagging doubt remained.

'Perhaps I ought to check that Fergus is all right?'

'For heaven's sake, leave it. He's OK!' Stella had kicked off her elegant little black pumps and had tucked her long velvet-trousered legs into her chair. Flora rested her feet on the warm fender and regretted that gardening seemed to have stiffened her joints rather than preserved their flexibility. It seemed unjust.

'But he's obviously really upset. It was such a shock –

about your father and that Kirsty woman. However did you find out about it?'

Stella laughed. 'You can be such a silly, Flora! I didn't!'

'You mean you just made it all up?'

'Mmm, but it just could be true. Unlikely though. But I wish I could really believe it; I'd like to think poor Daddy had some fun. Mother was such a selfish cold bitch!' If she heard Flora's shocked sharp intake of breath, Stella gave no sign of it.

'I did actually see them together once, you know, Daddy and Kirsty.' A dreamy tone had replaced the venom in Stella's voice. 'One evening, sitting at a little table in a dim corner of the lounge of the Station Hotel. Kirsty was wearing a silly little hat with a long pheasant's tail feather sticking up at the back. She looked just like a plump bird dressed for the table and Daddy was gazing at her as though he was longing to eat her up! I think she was drinking a port and lemon – I'm sure she would be!'

She's making it up, thought Flora, enthralled.

'Of course he pretended that he hadn't seen us – well, he would, wouldn't he? I was with Jimmy MacArthur; we were having a quick drink before the pictures. My word, I believed then that that was the height of racy sophisti-cation: a gin and orange in the Station Hotel and then off to the one and nines with a boyfriend! I thought all hell would be let loose later as Daddy had told me that I wasn't to go around with Jimmy who was "a fast-living young man with a well-deserved dubious reputation".' Stella smiled delightedly. 'Oh and he was . . . he was! But Daddy never said a word. Never let on.'

'But Stella, what's the point of saying these things to Fergus now, stirring things up? You *know* what he's like.'

'Yes, I do. That's why I said it. He's so insufferably pompous.' Stella's legs uncurled in one easy flowing motion, 'I'll just fetch what's left in the bottle.'

But when she padded back she was carrying a fresh bottle which she gripped between her knees as she drew the cork with an expertise that Flora considered a trifle reprehensible. But Stella is a career woman, she reminded herself by way of mitigation, and held out her glass. It had been the last bottle in the sideboard; Fergus had been keeping it for some special, although unspecified, occasion. I'll have to replace it before he notices, Flora told herself, and I must remember to put the empty right at the bottom of the dustbin.

'Fergus *needs* to be jolted now and again – don't you see that?' Stella's tone was crisp now, brooking no argument. 'God knows it's late in the day, but it's time he saw our parents as people – warts and all. He worshipped Mother, you know, and she had no time for him at all. Not that she had much time for anybody but herself.'

Flora felt vaguely uneasy. I shouldn't be listening to this, she thought. I do just what Stella is doing – rake over the past. But it should stay in one's head, not be voiced aloud. Shouldn't it?

'She seemed to dote on Bruce – but that wasn't love. Not really. It was more of a pride in an extension of herself. She thought he was the only one of her children worthy of her. Yes, that was it! It was always Bruce this and Bruce that, while Fergus mooched around like a puppy shut out in the cold. Do you know, when Bruce was shot down, Mother kept screaming, "What is there left for me to live for?"'

Stella paused and refilled her glass, holding the bottle first towards Flora who shook her head.

'Still, in all fairness, I suppose she was in such a state that she didn't realise what she was saying, or the effect of it. But Fergus never knew what it was that she expected of him, what he should do to gain her approval. So in the end he became impotent, frightened to try to make a success of anything in case he failed – at some level he realised that nothing would alter the way things were, you see.'

Stella fell silent, staring at the fire. Flora left to make the coffee.

She scrubbed at the pans in the sink as the coffee percolated, and tried not to think. On an impulse she abandoned the pans and ran upstairs to see how Fergus was. She moved quietly, more from fear of Stella hearing her than from anxiety not to disturb Fergus. He was asleep, his mouth slightly open, one arm flung over the coverlet; she tucked it gently under the blankets.

'Wonderful coffee!' Stella enthused. 'But then you

really are an awfully good cook, Flora. That dinner was simply superb.'

Flora smiled an acceptance of the compliment. I should feel pleased, she told herself, not somewhat diminished.

'Come along,' said Stella, draining her second cup, 'time we got off to bed.' She stood up and placed Flora's cup along with her own on the tray.

'But the dishes—' protested Flora.

'Oh, leave the bloody dishes! You look whacked out – probably my fault, indulging in melancholy trips down memory lane. It wasn't all doom and gloom, after all, the past.' Stella's voice was bright. How does she manage it, Flora wondered, trying to clamber out of her chair and her sombre mood.

'We had some good times. Better than most children have nowadays.'

They were upstairs, parting at Stella's door, when she added, 'Yes, there was a lot of fun – remember summers at Tangie Bay?'

'Well, I jolly well ought to! After all, that's how we got to know one another in the first place.' Flora's voice was a little dry. Stella's world, the Sinclair's world, had not been her world. Tangie Bay had been the only common factor.

The coffee had been a mistake, too strong and drunk too close to bedtime, Flora told herself, unable to get off to sleep. She had been so tired, so bone-tired, that she'd expected to drop off as soon as her head touched the pillow, Fergus's snoring notwithstanding.

I won't allow myself to think about the Sinclairs, nor about anyone else who belongs to the past. I won't, I won't, she instructed herself, giving her pillow a vicious punch.

If my brain refuses to shut down, then I'll occupy it with memories of Tangie Bay. The bay of the sea spirit. And it'll be memories of Tangie Bay before the Sinclairs came on the scene. No, that wouldn't be possible. They had always been on the scene although, initially, the two family groups, the Munros and the Sinclairs, had only politely and distantly acknowledged one another's presence. For years, summer after summer, they had preserved a separate identity, until that day at the Daisy Rock. But I won't let my memory take me that far, not tonight when I feel I've had more than enough of the Sinclairs, past and present.

Behind closed eyelids, Flora conjured up a memory of her Aunt Annie paddling in the shallows – gingham dress tucked into the elastic of her knickers; her legs, shorn of their beige lisle stockings, were white as suet where they were not blotched and veined with the winter's legacy of fire tartan. Annie's paddling had not been a sedate affair, she would hop and scream with mock terror as the larger waves slapped against her plump calves. In fact Tangie Bay wrought a change in Annie; on holiday there she became almost embarrassingly girlish, her physical

movements hoydenish as though her limbs, free of the
confines of the cramped villa in Abernethy Close, could
not quite adjust themselves to the wide expanse of beach
and moor. She was also, for these weeks, free of the
presence of her mother – old Mrs Munro being on her
annual visit to the spa at Strathpeffer whose waters, or so
she averred, did her rheumatism a power of good.

Agnes never wasted her time with the frivolity of paddling. Agnes in her sober woollen bathing suit went
swimming in the cove, prudently parallel to the shore
line, red-rubber-capped head bobbing up and down like a
float in time with the rhythm of each thrust of her slow,
strong breaststroke.

And Mother? Mother never entered the water but,
mindful of her complexion, would sit in the shadow of
the encircling sandstone cliff, a travelling rug beneath her
protecting both her art-silk dress from soiling and her
posterior from pile-inducing chill.

Her head pressed deep in her pillow, Flora imagined
she could hear the sea, but what she heard was only the
surge of her own blood. I wonder, she thought, if that is
why we are so entranced by the sea – the sound of it
echoes the beat of our hearts, the rhythmic flow of our
blood; perhaps it also evokes a reassuring memory of the
sounds that washed over and around us as we rocked in
the womb.

The water's roaring on wild days when the wind raced
in from the sea, its gentle lapping and hissing when the

day was so still that the heather and the harebells ceased to rustle and tremble – those were the sounds that filled the air at Tangie. The voice of the spirit of the sea. Even the thick stone walls of the cottage which they had rented were no proof against the noise of the sea. Flora could see it so clearly, the cottage that had been so quaintly named.

Peepie Cottage! A name guaranteed to produce a giggle in any child. The place where it stood had commanded such a good view of the approaches to the harbour that the women, in times past, would congregate there, shawls tightly wrapped round heads and shoulders, to 'take a peep' in the hope of an early sighting of the returning herring boats carrying their men safely back home.

The Munros had rented Peepie Cottage for a few weeks every summer. Their annual visit had been shorter than that of the migrant birds and yet the days spent under its grey slate roof were in some strange way more vivid in Flora's memory than were the years spent in her actual home.

The friction between her father's sisters, Agnes and Annie, and Flora's mother was very evident on these holidays when they were all confined under one roof. Despite their efforts to conceal their squabbles from Flora and their murmured reminders, one to the other, that 'little pitchers have long ears' there were, inevitably, occasions when Flora caught them off guard. Indeed, the charting of their running battle added a certain piquancy to Flora's enjoyment of these summer holidays; without that added excitement she, an only child restricted to the company of adults, might at times have found even the charms of the seaside wearing thin.

Peepie Cottage had only two bedrooms upstairs. In her teens Flora slept in a little room off the kitchen but when she was younger she shared the bedroom allocated to her aunts. It was there, bedroom walls and a tiny landing standing between themselves and Flora's mother, that Agnes and Annie would, in both senses of the words, let their hair down, quite unaware that their small niece was not always as soundly asleep as they assumed.

The light lingered so long on these summer evenings on that northern coast that the tardy dusk often merged with the dawn. But, sometimes, when the sky was overcast with dark rainclouds, the aunts would light the oil lamp on the dressing table when they came upstairs to retire to bed.

It may have been the pungent smell of the paraffin (Annie was apt to wind the wick downwards before applying the match and by the time she had seen her error the wick would be over-saturated), or it might have been the sudden light in the room which would awaken Flora on such occasions. But she would prudently lie still in her allotted place in the middle of the huge brass feather bed, feigning sleep, her eyelids not quite closed, her ears alert to the murmured conversation of her aunts and to the soft susurration of their clothes as these were systematically shed. Filtered through the fringe of her eyelashes, the golden light broke into a myriad of prisms and her aunts moved in a fragmented haze, their shadows weaving and converging in dark bulk on the low ceiling.

Agnes's movements were neat, economical; but then she had the advantage, as she drew off her stockings and unbuttoned her dress, of being able to sit on the one chair which the room afforded.

Annie hopped about in ungainly fashion as she divested herself of stockings and directoire knickers. The heat of her awkward efforts generated little sharp crackles of electricity as she hauled her pink rayon petticoat over her head. Eventually, clothed in her winceyette nightie, its limp linen buttons as yet undone in order to facilitate the ablutions yet to come, Annie would uncomplainingly await her turn at the washstand. Agnes, who favoured pyjamas – stout, striped garments – was scrupulous about using no more than her share of the hot water and would pause in her pouring to lift the lid of the brass can to check the amount still left in it.

Agnes's hair was swiftly dealt with. It seemed a pity that this rich and glossy chestnut asset should be so severely bobbed and its grooming so briefly effected by a few strokes from a hairbrush whose stiff wiry bristles were embedded in a cushion of bright pink rubber. Agnes had explained to Flora that hair that was short fitted more neatly under a nurse's cap and, besides, by the time Agnes could get to her bed at the end of a day on the wards she was far too tired to want to fiddle about with an elaborate hairstyle.

Annie's long hair was a sad dun colour and she wore it in plaited earphones. Such hairpins as still secured it after a day's shedding were now removed and the hair, once freed of its plaits, was carefully brushed before being constrained once more in a single heavy plait which hung down Annie's back. Annie brushed her hair with a seriousness and care which were somehow sad to Flora's watching eyes. She kept her hairbrush in a plywood box that was covered with brown and cream speckled lincrusta, which reminded Flora of chewed and spat-out nuts. Annie treasured that brush and its matching handmirror and clothes brush. Their backs were covered with irridescent butterfly wings, dark blue and gold, imprisoned under a transparent covering. The set had been a birthday present from her brother Duncan, Flora's father, who had over-estimated the demand for such exotic accessories when ordering his Christmas stock some years previously.

Hair attended to, the sisters would turn their attention to the care of their faces. Annie used Jonteel cold cream. Flora watched its diminishing level with a vested interest as she coveted the white porcelain jar on account of its label which bore a picture of a wonderful bird with a colourful curving tail. But Annie used the cream sparingly and applied it gently and lovingly, massaging it into her cheeks with circular movements, sweeping it upwards from her neck to her chin with firmly caressing fingertips. Flora could see from the reflection in the mirror that Annie's eyes were closed during this ritual and guessed that she was concentrating on remembering the step-by-step technique depicted in the diagrams on the page from *Home Chat* which her aunt kept in her drawer alongside her handkerchiefs.

Agnes kept her face cream in a round tin from which she gouged out a few dollops and almost flung them on to her face, vigorously scrubbing them into her sunburnt skin.

Before getting into bed, Annie kneeled by its side and, hands folded over freshly annointed and shining face, had a few private words with her Maker.

While this was going on, Agnes was already in occupancy of her side of the bed. But as Agnes, exuding a scent of lanoline and coal-tar soap, lay very still for a few minutes, Flora deduced that she, too, was saying her prayers and probably putting the Lord right about a few things – but with respect.

Perhaps the aunts felt that any conversation after that stage in the evening's procedures would be an anticlimax, or they may have been inhibited by the large framed text which hung on the wall opposite and adjured 'Judge not, that ye be not judged'; whatever the reason, the fact remained that they never chattered to one another once in bed, or not as far as Flora was aware – and it would have been difficult for her to remain unaware, sandwiched between them as she was until morning.

But it had been a different matter while they had been getting themselves ready for bed. That had been their talking time. There were random pauses and sometimes words had been muffled as clothes were drawn over faces, mouths blocked with toothbrushes, lips covered with face flannels, but a certain flow had been maintained.

Flora, lying now in the big walnut bed which Fergus had insisted on buying at the auction sale at Laggan Lodge, could hear the aunts almost as clearly as she had heard their voices in the bedroom of Peepie Cottage.

'What I find so unforgiveable, so downright *common*, is the way she never misses a chance to remind us that Duncan foots the bill for the holiday. Just loves rubbing it in!'

'But he *does* pay, Agnes, he pays the rent and pays Mrs Davidson to come in and do the cleaning and the cooking – there's no denying it.'

'And so well he might. It's the least he can do, if you ask me. What, I wonder, would happen to Mother if you didn't give up your life to looking after her? You did give up your teacher's training, after all – more fool you, some might think! It would cost him a pretty penny if he had to employ someone to do all that you do for her. And don't you forget that in return for inheriting everything worth having, he is *required to* make provision for Mother. Father wrote that in, remember.'

'But he does have a lot of calls on his purse, poor Duncan, when you come to think of it: Nelly to keep, Mother, Flora to bring up and you and me to support too, all out of the business.'

'He certainly does not support *me*!' Agnes's voice loud with indignation making Annie nervously shush her.

'Nelly may hear you.'

'Oh fiddle dee dee, I don't care if she does! That's another thing, she has a room to herself – no reason the child can't sleep there on a camp bed. It's not as though Duncan comes down every weekend. Great bed all to herself, selfish bitch!'

'Agnes!' Annie giggling and then glancing apprehensively towards the bed, mouthing something to her sister. Flora lying very quiet, resisting the give-away reaction of screwing her eyes tightly shut.

'I pay my share of the cost of the food, Annie – although I wouldn't be surprised if Duncan gives Nelly enough to cover it for all of us! The way she puts every damn thing down in that notebook of hers and then adds it all up and divides the total – even the peppermints for church, would you believe it!'

Her indignation spluttered into laughter and suddenly Agnes bent down, snatched the flower-painted chamber pot from beneath the bed and capered around the room chanting 'Put a penny in the poor man's pot'. She blundered into the spindly towel rack, sending it skittering across the linoleum and the pot would have crashed after it had not Annie, plait flying, swooped and caught it in time. Flora, aghast and fascinated, had forgotten her caution and sat up in bed, wide-eyed.

The aunts, sober now, turned towards her, Agnes still holding the chamber pot but with a comic dignity, like some ministering angel caught unaware.

Flora smiled now at the memory and, like a child who has been comforted by a bedtime story, could feel herself at last drifting into sleep. She was jerked back to wakefulness as Fergus switched on the light.

'What . . . are you all right, Fergus?'

'Oh, you're awake too, are you? I've scarcely slept a wink.'

'Is there anything I can get you?'

'No need for you to trouble yourself . . . although a couple of aspirin and a glass of water might help. My God, what a shambles of an evening. Stella's becoming more and more impossible. It's always the same with women: if they make a bit of money, get some power, they start throwing their weight around.'

Flora was returning from the bathroom when that deep doom-laden voice which she had overheard in the garden again reached her ears.

'Goodnight,' it said, and then intoned, '*Good* night? Ah! no; the hour is ill which severs those it should unite—'

Flora cautiously parted the curtains at the landing window. Below, one hand resting on the door handle of a car parked on Mr Hazel's drive, the other waving theatrically, drooped a rather weedy young man. Mr Hazel stood near him, toes inturned, smiling fatly and making the sort of farewell gesture one associated with the Queen Mother.

The car door slammed and Mr Hazel remained waving for a few seconds, his bald head shining in the glare of the retreating headlights.

Poor old chap, he does look lonely, thought Flora, as Mr Hazel turned and walked towards the light streaming from the back door which he had left wide open behind him.

But no, he wasn't alone after all! Flora could see a figure standing in the kitchen. My word, how late some of his guests stay, she thought with sympathy. The coated figure advanced towards Mr Hazel as he crossed the threshold. No, it wasn't wearing a coat, Flora screwed up her eyes the better to focus them; it was a bathrobe.

Suddenly the robe was flung wide and Flora saw that it had been wrapping a female form which now, for a brief and startling moment (the time it took for Mr Hazel to hide it from view in his arms), was revealed in all its pink nakedness.

Fergus had dropped off to sleep again.

Flora sat on the side of the bed and swallowed the aspirins and the water herself.

I just don't understand *anything*, she thought, flinging herself down on the bed like one who had been poleaxed.

4
~

'It's never as bad as it looks, it's just a matter of getting down to it.' That, reflected Flora, was the sort of bracing remark that sprang to the lips of a certain type of person – particularly in relation to domestic cleaning up. Part of growing older was discovering just how wrong people, including oneself, could be.

She slid the sideboard drawer shut on the best cutlery, now washed and dried, and turned to survey the dining room. The table had been cleared, the last hardened morsel had been scraped from the late Mrs Sinclair's Crown Derby and the tablecloth had been put to soak. But the atmosphere in the room was still heavy and not only with the lingering odour of food but with something else as well, something less tangible which the early morning air wafting from the opened window could not dispel.

Breakfast, she decided, would be eaten in the kitchen,

as and when Stella put in an appearance. Knowledge of the chores left undone had driven Flora downstairs early; she had worked quietly to the point of hindering her progress so as not to disturb the sleepers above.

She opened the front door and stood for a moment, milk bottles in hand, to gaze at the front garden. Gossamer, fine as a bride's veil, netted grass, shrubs and hedge, droplets of dew trapped in its mesh, sparkling like splintered glass.

It promised to be one of those cloudless, tranquil days that only Autumn can bestow, as though the best had been saved for the last. Even the honeysuckle that sprawled rampantly over the hedge, smothering and distorting its shape, a nagging reminder of gardening chores neglected, was transfigured into a delight to the eye with its crimson berries under the fine cobwebs winking like rubies set in spun silk.

On the other side of the hedge, looking rather chilly in her flimsy summer dress, the girl from the library scuttled down Mr Hazel's drive.

Flora closed the door sharply and leaned against it for a moment, agitated.

'Any hope of a cup of tea?' His voice unnecessarily loud, Fergus was standing on the landing, leaning over the bannisters, his hair ruffled like a coxcomb.

Later, at breakfast, Fergus seemed serene enough. He was wearing his favourite blue cashmere sweater and Flora,

82

surmising that this was unlikely to be in honour of their guest, took that as an indication that he felt fit enough to meet his cronies for their customary Sunday morning round of golf.

I could take Stella up on the Downs for a nice picnic lunch, she thought. With any luck, the unaccustomed fresh air will make her a bit torpid by evening and as that is also Fergus's normal state after his dinner the evening may well pass quite uneventfully, even pleasantly. The thought of an early retreat to bed at the end of it already seemed very attractive.

'Must see to my fish,' Fergus was dabbing at his moustache, pushing back his chair, 'so, if you'll excuse me.'

'Heavens, what an age he's taking over it!' Stella remarked some little time later as she helped Flora to clear away the breakfast things.

'He always does, but this morning I expect he'll take even longer – making up for last night when he was feeling too off-colour to do more than drop in their food.'

'But of course, I suppose that's why he didn't notice . . .'

Stella's sentence was not completed. Fergus had returned, was standing in the doorway and certainly had the air of someone who had noticed something – something like a tiger loose in the garden or the bailiffs on the doorstep.

'I can't believe it!' he said. 'At first I thought I was

seeing things.' He paused, and then, full realisation over-taking astonishment, he bawled, 'There's an *extra* fish in the tank!'

'That's right, a little surprise present – I was wonder-ing when you'd notice.'

Fergus stared at Stella.

'Are you saying that *you* put it there?'

Stella laughed a little uncertainly. Fergus was gripping the back of a chair, his knuckles white.

'There's a new pet shop just opened up near my flat. They've masses of the most beautiful fish there, the only shop I've seen with marine fish as well as the usual fresh-water tropicals. I thought it might be tricky carrying a fish in the car but the man just popped it into a poly-thene bag – I was terrified it might burst!' Stella was rattling on, a little nervously, in the face of Fergus's omi-nous silence. 'They were all so beautiful, I had quite a job choosing, but I thought the one I settled on was so pretty, that gorgeous rose colour and golden fins . . .'

'I suppose it didn't occur to you to think about *Oodinium* or *Ichthyopthirius*?' Fergus's voice was unnatu-rally quiet.

'Well, actually I think that one is called a Rose Clown, of course it probably has a more scientific name as well. But I don't think the man mentioned . . . what was it, you said, *Oodinium*?'

'You bloody fool, I'm talking about *diseases*, not types of fish! Don't you know *anything*? Not a fish, not a piece of coral or a plant goes into my aquarium before it's spent fourteen days in quarantine in a copper sulphate solution.'

Flora found herself nodding. 'That's right, Stella, it's in the boxroom, the quarantine tank.'

Fergus waited with exaggerated patience for Flora to finish.

'And now *you* place in my aquarium some interloper of unknown origins to hazard *my fish*!'

'Oh Fergus, I'm sure the little chap's in good condition – it is a very exclusive sort of shop, not just any old place.'

Fergus snorted. 'Just because you probably paid over the odds for it, doesn't prevent it bringing disease into my tank, although I'm not surprised that that should be your line of reasoning.'

Stella attempted to say something but Fergus wagged a finger close to her face and shouted, 'I haven't finished yet.' Having quashed any risk of interruption, he continued in a hectoring tone. 'Quite apart from the fact that your wretched fish might have already been harbouring a disease when you bought it, don't you realise that *any* fish may come out in white spot with the chill and stress of disturbance and then spread the disease to healthy valuable fish?' Fergus in his increasing agitation had advanced further on Stella and now, his face only inches away from hers, roared, 'You stupid interfering cow – don't you know what you've done?'

He raised his arm. Stella took a step backwards but Fergus only dragged his hand over his head and brought it to rest clutched over his eyes.

'Look, Fergus, how was I to know? I've said I'm sorry and I am. But you've no right to bawl and shout at me – when all's said and done, it's only a matter of a few ruddy fish.'

Flora retreated into the scullery.

She experienced an almost overwhelming urge to run; she had a brief vision of herself racing down the lane, screaming. But the screaming was coming from the kitchen, they were going at one another hammer and tongs, insults flying, old grievances and jealousies were torn up by the roots and hurled from one to the other. Flora put her hands over her ears

A door banged. More faintly, from upstairs, came the sound of another door slamming shut.

The kitchen was empty when Flora crept back from the scullery, her knees trembling and so weak that the thought that they might have borne her, running, away seemed ludicrous.

She could hear water running upstairs in the bathroom, crashing into a bucket. Fergus must be filling the quarantine tank. And where was Stella?

Stella, as Flora discovered when she felt able to climb the stairs to investigate, was in her room, packing.

'I'm off!' she said, glancing up from the open case on the bed.

'Oh Stella, I'm so sorry – it's all such a silly storm in a teacup.' Flora could hear her voice quavering.

Stella's tight-lipped expression melted to a grin, 'Splash in a tank, more like! Come on, let's have a quick snifter to buck us up.'

'Yes, yes, of course, I'll fetch . . .' Flora moved back towards the door, but hesitantly, fearing to meet Fergus whom she had just heard going downstairs.

'No, don't go away. I've got a flask.' Stella had pulled a flask from her overnight bag and was pouring a measure of whisky into its silver cap and splashing another into the tooth-glass which she'd taken from the washbasin.

'Goodness, you're prepared for everything.'

'Well, we unmarried women have to be self-sufficient – no men dancing attendance on us, y'know.'

Did Stella really think marriage was like that, or was there an ironic edge to her voice? Uncertain, Flora said nothing but sat down on the bed beside her sister-in-law.

'Do you know, Flora, when I was in that pet shop, there was a chap there buying an aquarium and some fish for a friend of his. He said this friend had recently lost his wife, so he wanted to give him something to take his mind off it. The man in the shop sold him four goldfish and a couple of orfe. Now isn't that a salutary thought. It's my guess that Fergus would reckon that a couple of guppy would well compensate for my demise.'

Flora laughed, a trifle hysterically, and then, abruptly sobered, said, 'He didn't really mean those awful things he said, Stella. Fergus has been a bit odd recently, edgy. Perhaps it's the effect of retirement or having time to look back . . . to look back and find nothing much behind him, just empty corridors. Sorry if that sounds fanciful. He's started to dramatise himself to make up for it. At least, I think that's what he's doing. He's drinking more than he ought to, it can't be doing his liver any good. And then there's . . . oh, but it's impossible to explain, perhaps I'm making too much out of things. I'm baffled about most things these days, perhaps I always have been. Will you be all right for a bed tonight?'

'No hassle, dear! I'll book in at the Airport Hotel. Much more convenient, actually, for an early flight – saves me making a start from here at some ungodly hour.'

'Honestly, Stella, I can't tell you how vexed I am about it all. I know you put yourself out to come and see us . . . and now . . . and I was so looking forward to having you to talk to.'

'Well, can't be helped. What was it your formidable Aunt Agnes used to say? "Greater loss at Culloden!"'

'So she did! D'you know, I'd almost forgotten that. Never found it much of a comfort myself. But how did you know that she used to say that?'

'I heard her that morning at the Daisy Rock. Mother seemed a trifle reluctant about her silk scarf being ripped up for emergency bandaging.'

'I thought you were unconscious.'

'So I had been, but I did come round eventually – more or less. I can't remember all that much, but that phrase impinged somehow – I'd never heard it before.'

'Stella, there's another thing I don't understand . . .'

'What?'

'Well, I can see how you could, well, sort of harbour a resentment towards Fergus because you're indebted to him – after all he did save your life and risked his own at the Daisy Rock.' Flora said it quickly, embarrassed at what might be construed by Stella as a crass reminder of a debt of gratitude. 'But it doesn't make any sense that Fergus should be so resentful towards you. The jealousy, that I understand; you've achieved so much more with your life than Fergus. But jealousy doesn't account for all of it – does it? Somehow, it doesn't seem to add up.'

'No?' Stella was gathering up her toothbrush, face cream, comb, putting them away in her sponge bag. She's not really giving any attention to what I'm saying, thought Flora, her mind is already away from here – concerned with her business, the meeting in Switzerland, the journey ahead.

'Try this for size then.' Stella had turned towards Flora again. 'Supposing what he did at the Daisy Rock gave Fergus heroic expectations of himself, and perhaps others shared those expectations – what then, if he found he couldn't sustain the role thrust upon him? Perhaps he'd then begin to wish that that incident had never happened at all, would come to hate even the memory of it – and me, too, of course! There you are, dear, instant psychoanalysis, QED.' Stella laughed, but a little self-consciously.

Flora said nothing and shook her head as Stella extended the flask towards her once more. Stella screwed the silver top back in place and stuffed the flask in her bag.

'Why go looking for complicated answers? Fergus is what he is because he's Fergus. He's self-important, self-righteous, self-pitying and snobbish – my God, he isn't even unique!' She was crushing down the contents of her bag with jerky, impatient thrusts, struggling to close the zip. 'Sorry, Flora, I shouldn't have said all that.'

She slung the strap of her bag over her shoulder, closed her case and picked it up, glanced quickly round the room but not at Flora.

'Time I was off – before I plant my big foot in it any deeper.'

Flora followed behind her down the stairs, her guilt that she was carrying nothing tempered by her envy of Stella who was clearly capable of carrying her own luggage unaided.

Fergus didn't come to the door as Stella drove away.

Flora stood for some minutes alone by the gate, looking down the lane long after Stella was out of sight.

5
~

Flora wished now that she hadn't brought the bowl of roses into the sitting room. She had thought it a pity that their beauty should be wasted in the empty dining room, but their sweet scent heavy on the air gave the room even more of the atmosphere of a funeral parlour.

Her eyes were drawn irresistibly to the corner where the aquarium stood. The tank was shrouded in black polythene and its mute and sombre presence dominated the room, it being no more capable of being overlooked than would have been a coffin. In one of Fergus's brief absences from its side, Flora had peeped under the covering and been shocked to discover that the water was dark, almost opaque, the fish scarcely visible. Unreasonably, she had found herself grieving the absence of the enigmatic stare of the little mandarin.

The sound of her knitting needles struck her as being loud in the hush of the room, their busy clack somehow callous. But I have to do *something*, she told herself, wondering how Fergus could just sit there, so silent and listless now that he could find nothing more to say about Stella's folly. He sat in his accustomed place, armchair so positioned that a turn of his head to the right afforded him a full view of his aquarium while the television met his gaze when he chose to look straight ahead. He had, as was his custom, switched the set on as soon as he had sat down, but had turned the sound so low that even the bubbling of the aerator in the tank could be heard distinctly above it.

'The aerator seems unusually noisy,' she ventured, her voice pitched low as seemed appropriate to the circumstances.

'It is. I've increased the aeration as well as dropping the temperature.'

'Really! I thought that you'd covered the tank up to raise the temperature.'

'No, no. The tank has to be kept in darkness during the treatment.'

'Ah.' Flora completed a row and then let the pins lie idle on her lap so that Fergus would not guess that her interest was superficial.

'How long will it be before you know . . .'

'Impossible to tell. Methylene Blue isn't infallible, you know. I added the second dose today, twenty-four hours after the first. Can't do more now – it's just a question of waiting.'

Flora nodded and, after a decent interval during which Fergus showed no inclination to say more, she picked up her knitting again.

Later, while Fergus was upstairs checking the condition of the Rose Clown in the quarantine tank, Letty rang.

'Is Fergus there? I'd like a word.' she said, after the briefest acknowledgement of Flora's presence at the other end of the line.

'He's not available at the moment. Remember, Stella arrived on Saturday to visit us.' That, after all, was true; if Letty understood her to mean that Stella was still with them and that she and Fergus were out somewhere together, then that would be Letty's misconstruction.

'I may not be able to ring later,' said Letty after a slight hesitation. 'I've seized my chance while Eleanor's out settling Nicholas Nye down for the night.'

'Could I be of help?'

'Well . . .' there was a degree of doubt in Letty's voice which Flora found less than flattering.

'It's like this – I have to go up to London tomorrow on an early train to meet an old cousin who's coming down from Scotland. She's going into hospital for an op and wants me to hold her hand. Anyway, I'll have to stay over for a couple of nights; won't be back before Thursday morning.'

'Oh yes?' Flora cautious now, remembering something once said about Eleanor being terrified of being alone at night; stupid woman!

'I expect you know how it is with Eleanor . . . too silly, but she can't help it. She really is absolutely terrified of being alone in the house after dark. That's why I was wondering . . .' Letty let her voice tail off.

If she thinks, thought Flora. Oh no, Eleanor's not coming here and Fergus is most certainly not going *there*!

Meeting silence, Letty had no option but to break it. 'I suggested that she comes with me, but she won't. Actually, I don't think she wants to admit . . . well, one can understand it. Besides, I think she hopes that I won't go, won't leave her on her own – but I *must*, you see. Do you think – I know it's asking a lot, but could you possibly—'

Flora interrupted before she could be manoeuvred into too specific a commitment.

'If you have to, then you must go, Letty. I'm sure you don't need to worry about anything.'

'I knew you'd understand. Thanks awfully. Must ring off now, Eleanor'll be back any moment. Bye!'

I wonder what she thinks she's thanking me for, Flora thought, feeling a quiet sense of triumph that she had succeeded in outsmarting Letty.

Fergus, impossible though that might have seemed, was even more deeply sunk in gloom when he came downstairs. The Rose Clown had come out in spots and the likelihood was now high that during its twenty-four hours in the aquarium it would have infected the other fish. Flora told herself that this was no time to add to his burden of anxiety.

They were getting ready for bed when Fergus remarked that he'd heard the phone ringing earlier in the evening.

'Oh that – just Letty. Going up to London for a couple of days apparently. Just thought she'd let us know.'

'Ah – Eleanor did mention they might take a break soon for a few days – do some shopping, see some shows. I was going round tomorrow to help them move some furniture; they want the carpet taken up and sent to the cleaners – that bloody dog y'know! Well, just as well that's cancelled as I need to keep a close watch on the fish for the next few days.'

Flora devoted the next day to working outside. It was high time, she told herself, that the front garden was given some attention and if, while she was working there, she was also ideally placed to circumvent a visit from Eleanor, then that was purely fortuitous. She didn't know quite how she would prevent Eleanor from entering the house but, having discovered her unexpected talent for dissimulation, had no doubt that something appropriate would occur to her should the need arise.

She clipped the cotoneaster, dug out the honeysuckle and cut back the aubretia. As she worked she could feel the tension coursing from her along with the trickles of sweat that ran down her body. A host of twittering housemartins swooped and tumbled high in the sky like a cloud of midges. They're getting ready to leave, Flora thought, leaning on her spade and squinting up at them, and felt comforted by this evidence of the ineluctable pattern of the seasons which affirmed that nothing lasts forever.

Fergus's day, closeted in the house brooding over his fish, had failed to bestow upon him any such homely philosophical insight. Flora found herself hard put to it to maintain a modicum of cheerfulness in the face of his morose presence at the dinner table. Perhaps fish, even when masked with parsley sauce, had not been the most tactful choice of dish to set before him. Fergus pushed his portion around his plate with a marked lack of enthusiasm.

In the course of the afternoon one of the precious long-nosed butterfly fish and a pair of blue damsels had expired. In a voice laden with doom, Fergus confided that he dreaded to think what the toll might be in the coming hours.

Flora struggled with a wild desire to giggle; the urge was similar to that which had plagued her as a child when confronted by adult solemnity. It is *not* funny, she instructed herself sternly; his fish mean a great deal to Fergus and just because he seemed, in her view, to be overreacting to their present plight, that in no way lessened his distress. But still the errant giggle trembled in her throat, brooking no suppression. When it finally succeeded in bursting free, Flora managed to transform it into a strange yelping cough. The tears that brimmed over her lashes were impossible to disguise but Fergus, seeing them, patted her hand sympathetically.

'Never mind, old thing, we've weathered worse together,' he said by way of comfort. Flora's sobriety was instantly restored.

Until the squamous melodrama had been resolved, one way or another, the thought of keeping Fergus company in his vigil by the shrouded aquarium in the sitting room was untenable.

Flora brought her sewing machine into the kitchen and spent the evening sides-to-middling sheets, a chore so uncongenial that it reduced, a little, her feelings of guilt about her own lack of sympathy towards Fergus. When, around midnight, Fergus still showed no signs of taking himself off to bed and not a sheet remained which required her attention, Flora completed her self-abnegation by replacing all the missing buttons on his shirts.

From a distance there came the sound of Nicholas Nye braying. Well, thought Flora, snapping off a thread with her teeth, at least Eleanor does not entirely lack for company.

6
~

'I'm just off to the pub.'

Flora didn't look round; she was stirring a pan of lemon curd on the stove and it had reached the critical stage when it trembled on the edge of boiling, and that it must not be permitted to do.

'All right, dear.'

Fergus was already opening the front door when Flora hastily pulled the pan to one side and rushed after him.

'You'll need to get petrol; I noticed this morning that the tank's nearly empty.'

'I'm not taking the car.' Fergus's voice sounded dispirited and he looked slightly unkempt, perhaps only because his moustache was untrimmed and his jacket had the misaligned appearance of a garment which had been carelessly shrugged into rather than donned with confidence.

'That's a good idea – the walk will perk you up, you'll

see.' Flora stood and waved him off but he didn't look back.

He's going to get drunk, she thought, and that's why he's not taking the car. Wednesday was not one of his pub nights, but then his routine had been in complete disarray ever since Sunday and his subsequent total pre-occupation with his aquarium. At least, Flora thought, pouring the curd into the warmed jars, I've known what was occupying his mind over the last few days and that made a change.

The jars covered and labelled, there was nothing to keep her in the kitchen. Too early to go to bed, she decided. Waiting for Fergus to return she would, in any case, be unable to fall asleep. She dreaded to think about what state he might be in when he came home but, judging from past experience of his occasional binges, he'd need her assistance, if only to get undressed. I'm no Letty, she thought, fiercely resentful of Letty's calm competence in dealing with Eleanor's lapses. Flora had once insinuated to Letty that perhaps she could prevent Eleanor from over-indulging, might even attempt to cure her of the habit. 'Not if she doesn't want to come off drink! In any case that's her way of getting through life – it's not up to me to interfere,' Letty had said. She hadn't actually told Flora, not in so many words, to mind her own business; but it had been implicit. But, Flora assured herself briskly, Fergus is not an alcoholic like Eleanor, he only has occasional lapses when things get too much for him. She comforted herself with the knowledge that in an excess of post-alcoholic remorse and self-disgust he'd be sweet reasonableness personified for the remainder of the week. If I pick my moment, she promised herself, I'll be able to have a reasonable talk with him – and not let him get away with any of his usual 'it's all right, pro tem' nonsense.

She switched on the television and dragged an arm-chair into a position from which the aquarium was not visible. The black polythene had been removed, but nothing stirred in the dark water. The last surviving fish, two harlequins and the little mandarin, had floated to the surface, dead, shortly after dinner. The Rose Clown, Stella's fatal gift, had shown signs of recovery in the quarantine tank, but Fergus had lifted it out and flushed it down the lavatory.

I could get up and switch channels, but I can't be bothered, thought Flora, as a series of heads lectured her on the possibility, or was it the impossibility, of a nuclear war. A group of women, at least she assumed they were women although there were few certainties left to her, appeared briefly; they seemed to be hanging various articles of apparel on to the mesh of a high fence. Tony Benn swam into focus and fixed her with a baleful eye. Another glass tank, another mandarin, she thought as her eyelids drooped. But Fergus's Clowns had been prettier.

Flora was awakened by the high-pitched whine coming

from the television set whose screen was now as blank as the aquarium behind her. Dazed, she glanced at the clock and discovered that it was well past midnight.

She rose and stumbled to the set, one leg tingling with pins and needles. She turned the set off and the ensuing silence seemed ominously absolute.

Fergus's jacket and fore-and-aft were not hanging on the hall stand but that, she told herself, didn't necessarily signify that he had not returned. She ran upstairs, half-expecting to find him on the bed, fully dressed.

The bedroom was empty, pristine, waiting. She stood, one hand resting on the doorknob, fully awake now but her brain obstinately refusing to function efficiently. She turned and went slowly downstairs away from the silence of the bedroom and headed for the kitchen where the murmur of the refrigerator and the drip of the scullery tap seemed suddenly reassuring.

I ought to phone someone . . . the hospital, the police? But perhaps someone had tried to telephone me while I was asleep and the television on. Fergus might have rung. That could be it! Fergus might have met one of his pals at the pub, gone home with him (her?) at closing time . . .

She went into the hall, flicked over the dog-eared pages of the notebook by the telephone, then closed it. She would sound such a fool, ringing the Clares, the Greens or any other of Fergus's golfing friends to ask them (and at this late hour) if Fergus was with them. It wasn't even as though she really knew any of them, at least not well enough to make the enquiry sound sprightly, offhand.

I shouldn't have let him go off alone, not in the state he was in, she told herself, agitated now. 'In sickness and in health' – and Fergus is sick, in a strange sort of way.

A car was coming up the drive, crunching over the gravel. A door slammed. She heard voices, male, calm.

She was already standing on the doorstep as they came into view; two policemen with Fergus between them, his colour ghastly in the light of the blue lamp that flickered from the roof of the car.

Fergus heaved himself up on the pillows.

'You shouldn't have bothered. I'll be getting up in half an hour or so.'

Flora placed the tray on his knees. 'Black coffee and melba toast – all right?'

'Yes, just the thing!' Shamefaced, Fergus avoided her eyes, poured a cup of coffee, his hand trembling a little.

'How do you feel – you did sleep quite soundly?' Flora herself had slept in the spare room – if one could call it sleeping; she'd looked in on the comatose Fergus several times during the small hours.

'I'll be OK. This stings a bit though.' Fergus fingered the plaster across his nose. 'A few stitches under that, I think; and there's a bruise or two giving me gyp. Still, could be worse!'

'I still don't understand how you came to be in Eleanor's car.'

'No?'

'Well the policemen – they were such nice boys, I thought – they only told me that there'd been an accident; the car had collided with a cyclist and ended up in the ditch. You'd all been taken to hospital but only 'the lady' had been kept in. You, of course, were in no state to tell me anything much.'

'Yes . . . well, I don't remember much about it, actually.'

'But you must remember what you were doing in her car in the first place – with Eleanor, I mean. You told me you were walking down to the pub.'

'That was where I went, to the pub. I was thinking about leaving, it was not long to closing time and I thought I'd catch that bus that passes the end of the lane, save on a taxi fare, y'see.'

'And?' Flora persisted, her dislike of badgering Fergus while he looked so defenceless lending an angry edge to her voice. But, she told herself, if I don't get it out of him now, then I'll never get at the truth; when he has his wits properly about him, he'll bamboozle me.

'I'm telling you. That's when Eleanor walked into the pub.' He was crumbling the toast between his fingers. 'I don't think I can manage this, perhaps later.'

'But what on earth was Eleanor doing there – and at that time of night?'

'Must say it floored me – seeing her there; thought she and Letty were up in town. She was a bit . . . well—'

'Drunk?'

Fergus frowned. 'In an emotional state, so to speak. Anyway, she'd run out of gin and had come down to the pub to buy a bottle, or two. Couldn't get through the night alone cold sober. Not that she was what you might call cold sober.' Fergus put his hand to his head and groaned. 'We chatted a bit. She had the car, I was on my way home, so it seemed the natural thing to do, to go home together.'

'But Fergus, what on earth were you thinking about – taking a lift home with her in that state?' And you little better, thought Flora, realising that she'd arrived at the answer to her own question.

'You're so right Flora dear, so right – it was damned silly. I should have rung for a taxi – but you know how it is, hindsight and all that.'

'Well, she's in real trouble now – drunken driving, and I doubt if it's for the first time. Causing an accident! My God, Fergus, that poor cyclist could have been killed; Eleanor might well be facing a manslaughter charge. You can just thank your lucky stars . . . Did they breathalyse you as well?'

Fergus had both his hands on his head now.

'Yes, yes, yes! Look Flora, for God's sake leave it will you? Just leave it!'

She jerked the tray away. At the door she paused,

tempted to fire a parting shot while she had the advantage. Her anger began to evaporate in the face of Fergus's woebegone appearance: one side of his pyjama collar poked upwards, incongruously; she must have buttoned him into it lopsidedly.

'Look Flora, I've said I'm sorry – or, if I haven't, then I'm saying it now. Pax, eh?'

Embarrassed by the schoolboyish appeal, she looked down at the tray with its broken toast, puddle of spilt coffee.

'I'll ring the hospital and find out how Eleanor is.'

She was out of the room, the door banging sharply behind her, before he could reply.

He was downstairs by eleven. Showered, shaved, smelling of Brut, not quite meeting her eye, his hands restless, tweaking at his tie, pulling at the hem of his pullover. He's pulling his tattered dignity together, Flora thought, he'll have it cobbled together by nightfall. She kept him waiting, not telling him what she knew he must want to hear, until he was forced to ask.

'You rang the hospital, did you?'

'Yes. She's comfortable, the sister said. Well, they always say that, don't they, unless the patient's actually dead!'

'What about . . . well, visitors?'

'She's had one of those. Letty got back late last night, it seems. She's been to the hospital already. I expect she brought Eleanor everything she needs; seen to things.'

'Good, good. But what I meant was, can she see visitors yet – other than Letty, I mean.'

'Not before tomorrow afternoon. So I'll go then, after lunch. You'd best stay here – take things quietly for a few days.'

Fergus looked relieved. Flora hadn't expected that.

'Yes, perhaps that'd be best. Eleanor'd prefer that, I expect. Shouldn't think she'd want a man around, not while she's under the weather. I'll just go and see to the aquarium, empty it and so forth. No good crying over spilt milk!'

That, thought Flora, is something gained, surely. Perhaps he needed something like this to happen to bring him to his senses, restore his sense of proportion.

She went upstairs to make the bed, fling the windows wide. She was quite looking forward to the prospect of dealing with Eleanor the next day, a chastened bed-fast Eleanor.

7
~

'Look darling, I'm all dressed up to do the Charleston!'
Eleanor lifted one thin hand to the bandage that encircled
her forehead. Her other hand was almost entirely encased
in the plaster that extended over her forearm as far as the
elbow joint; only her finger tips peeped out, their nakedness disturbing, like the resting claws of some burrowing
creature caught at a disadvantage above ground.

She looks ghastly, thought Flora, disappointed that
she experienced no satisfaction from that observation.
Her face, dingy below the stark whiteness of the head
bandage, was reminiscent of a dried-out shammy leather.
Deep in the crumpled folds her eyes glittered, feverishly
bright. I refuse to feel sorry for her. Flora looked quickly
away. Drunken fool, she could have killed Fergus and
that poor old fellow on his bike.

'Nice room.' Flora was relieved to find something to
say which was free of the taint of hypocrisy. It really was

a pleasant room: fitted carpet, bright chintz curtains; more like an hotel room than a hospital ward, she thought. Trust Eleanor to land on her feet – metaphorically at least. The only other bed in the room was empty, but the presence of cards and flowers on the locker beside it suggested that that was only a temporary state of affairs.

'It's not too bad, I suppose. I'd have preferred a single, naturally, but I suppose this is the next best thing. The old girl in the other bed's had a stroke, so she's down in therapy most of the time. Can't talk so that's a great blessing!'

'Fergus asked me to bring you this, he thought it might cheer you up.' Eleanor stretched out her hand for the book and glanced at its faded spine. 'Oh! *Night Life of the Gods*, what fun! Do tell him, it's *absolutely* right. How one *adored* Thorne Smith!' Flora hadn't, but forbore to say so.

'And I brought you some pears – our own Conference.' Flora was busying herself in trying to fit them into the overflowing fruit bowl and contriving to mask their homeliness as much as possible with the black grapes that crowned the choice pile.

'They're just ready to eat – I've been keeping them in a drawer. They're not windfalls,' she added, a trifle defensively. 'Would you like me to peel one for you?'

'Not just now dear, but I'm sure they're lovely. Could you just lift the grapes a little, I'd hate them to get bruised. Letty brought them this morning, at the crack, my dear. She knows how I love them. She thinks of everything, dear old stick! I rather fancy one now – could you possibly?'

Flora broke off a small sprig and turned to place it in Eleanor's hand but was disconcerted to see that Eleanor's eyes were closed and her mouth open to receive delicate sustenance. How unpleasantly intimate, she thought, popping a grape between the parted lips and withdrawing her fingers sharply, dreading the touch of saliva.

At close quarters, Eleanor smelt of expensive scent and antiseptic. 'Chanel,' said Flora, unthinkingly, as a shadow of her father's shop was evoked by the miasma.

'Yes! Goodness, fancy you recognising that!'

Eleanor's breasts, unfettered below the apricot silk nightdress, were pendulous, the skin, visible in the lace-bordered 'V', large pored. Like a plucked turkey, thought Flora, surreptitiously wiping her fingers on the counterpane.

'Dear Fergus all right?'

'Not too bad. But a shock for a man of his age, of course! He didn't feel up to coming to visit you,' Flora answered, primly.

'You were right to keep him at home, Flora. Much the best thing!'

'Must have given Letty a terrible shock too.'

'Yes, I suppose it did – but she's awfully good in a crisis. Positively blossoms – quite the Girl Guide manqué! I suppose nothing ever surprises Letty – bless her! She arrived home on the last train, found the police's note stuck in the letter box. Her taxi was still turning round in the drive so she just hopped back in and was round here straight away. They'd only just got me patched up and into bed when she arrived. She'd have stayed here the rest of the night but that bloody sister wouldn't have it.

'She's already sent a cable off to Alastair, you know!' Eleanor grinned. '"Eleanor in hospital stop drunken driving charge stop accident victim holding his own stop"!' Eleanor was laughing and then ceased abruptly on a sharp intake of breath.

'Oh God, that hurts,' she gingerly caressed her chest. 'Ribs bruised y'know. I'd give anything to see Alastair's face – he's in the US of A staying with his precious Melanie and her dreary parents at Cape Cod. Can you imagine his face when that drops into the idyll! Letty can be positively inspired at times.'

'But the man on the bike – I thought he was unhurt? At least the police said . . .'

'Yes, He's OK. But it's true, he was certainly "holding his own" when I saw him – at least nobody else could possibly lay claim to it! Bicycles can do vicious things to a man if company is suddenly parted, y'know!'

Eleanor was laughing again, but more cautiously this time, her lips together, snorting through her nose.

She has no sense of shame whatsoever, thought Flora,

conscious that the visit was not turning out at all as she had imagined it. She felt an alarming urge to slap Eleanor, to scream at her. She turned and buried her face in the vase of roses on the bedside locker, concerned to hide her mounting flush of anger.

'What lovely roses,' she murmured, her face still turned away from the bed. They had no scent but that was not to be wondered at, not in that modern perfectly formed style of bloom where scent was so often sacrificed in favour of appearance. No rose scent, Flora sniffed again, suspiciously: but there was certainly a smell of something.

'Letty brought them. Of course they're not real – made of silk, actually.'

Eleanor wriggled herself a little higher on the pillows and stretched out her arm.

'Pour me a little drinky, darling, it's so damned awkward with only one hand.'

Flora reached for the carafe.

'No, no! From the flower vase, silly!'

Flora looked dazedly at the roses.

'Oh, for God's sake, Flora – whoever heard of artificial flowers needing water! They're standing in gin. I told you, Letty thinks of everything. Do hurry up!'

Flora did as she was told.

'Now just a weeny splash of tonic – there's a bottle in the locker.'

Eleanor, tumbler in hand, leaned back and sighed. 'That's better,' she said, comfortably. 'It does have a certain *je ne sais quoi* – the flower stems, I suppose, but beggars can't be choosers.'

Flora glanced uneasily towards the door. 'What if a nurse comes in?'

'Not to worry! One of the advantages of a private ward is that the staff hardly bother with one – they don't approve of privilege, you see. Of course I do believe it should be spread around a bit – privilege, I mean. Well, I do what I can. I'll be giving Alastair the privilege of paying for all of this.' Eleanor waved her already nearly empty glass to indicate the room. 'And then there'll be the fine – that'll be a whopper, I should think. They'll probably take my licence away too, but I shouldn't worry. Letty generally drives me around anyway; no good keeping a dog and barking yourself. I suppose one could say that all this business is Letty's fault really. If she'd been where she ought to have been, then none of it would have happened.' She gave Flora a sidelong look. 'I suppose that isn't really fair, blaming Letty. But then it's always a great comfort to blame someone else – isn't it?'

She thrust the glass towards Flora. 'Just a little top up, darling!'

Well, it's her funeral, thought Flora, hoping it might well be and recklessly filling the glass to the brim.

'I ought to be getting back to Fergus.'

'Ah, dear Fergus! You don't know how lucky you are, Flora, having a man like that. He's so kind – not many men like him around. Look at the way he buried himself in that dreary school so that you could enjoy a sort of surrogate family. Although why anyone should grieve over not having brats, I can't imagine!'

'Did he tell you that?'

Eleanor shrugged. 'Perhaps not in so many words. But one can put two and two together.'

It's the gin, thought Flora, feeling under her chair for her handbag. I don't have to sit here listening to this maudlin nonsense.

But Eleanor had not yet finished.

'Yes, some people have all the luck. Now me – everything and everyone I ever coveted either belonged to someone else or was taken from me.'

Tears had gathered in Eleanor's eyes. 'I just don't know how I'm going to face being without him. I could always talk to him in a way I couldn't with anyone else. He never did anyone any harm, dear, useless, stupid old thing . . .' Her voice tailed off into a little wail.

How dared she! I can think these things, but that she should . . . Flora's furious glare was wasted on Eleanor who was now openly weeping, her hand fumbling blindly for the box of tissues on the locker.

Flora thrust a tissue into her hand. I daren't ring for the nurse, she thought, she'll blame me; they've probably got her on some drug that is interacting with the gin – oh, what a mess! She was on her feet, ready to make a dash for the door while Eleanor was still busy mopping her eyes.

As though sensing her intention, Eleanor suddenly reached out and grasped Flora's wrist, the soggy tissue still in her hand.

Flora was trying to tug her wrist free, very conscious of the warm wet tissue, but Eleanor's grip was firm.

'No, don't go Flora!' Her voice was quite steady now. 'Sorry about that, I think I must still be a bit muzzy.

'I know you think I'm a silly, selfish bitch – most people do. They're probably right. Do you know, when I was a girl I really thought the world was going to be my oyster! Well, it didn't turn out quite like that. I guess I'm just one of the bits of grit that never becomes a pearl, and that wasn't at all what I had in mind for myself.'

She released her grip and Flora scrubbed at her wrist with her handkerchief, not looking at Eleanor.

'Oh, what the hell! "That's how the cookie crumbles" as our transatlantic cousins put it – I wonder if Melanie says things like that? I expect Alastair deserves her, I always suspected that there was a vulgar streak in him – a taint of the bourgeois. Mother did warn me that a man who wore sock-suspenders was suspect!' Eleanor laughed.

'But now, now Flora, I rather fancy being a pearl. Temporarily naturally. I want Fergus to be quite sure about something but with my hand in plaster I can't write to him, so you'll have to give him a message.'

Eleanor's voice was on the verge of slurring so she was enunciating her words with pedantic care.

'Just you tell him that my mind is quite made up and

I'm sticking to my guns. You could say that the lady's not for turning!'

'I don't know what you're talking about.'

'No? Well it doesn't matter – but you tell Fergus that and he'll understand.'

Seeing Flora's expression of open-mouthed disbelief that she should be used as a go-between, Eleanor smiled.

'I do believe that you do understand what I'm on about. Just indulge my sudden desire for magna . . . magna thingamabob. "You know it makes sense" as that other lady who is not for turning is fond of saying – and she generally gets her own way.'

Flora could not trust herself to say anything.

'Now, be a dear girl and hand me a couple of pepper-mints – there's a bag in the locker. Oh, and you'd better give the glass a rinse while you're at it. You don't want sister after you as an accessory to the crime, as it were.'

Flora found the peppermints and placed the bag on the coverlet within Eleanor's reach and then sat gazing wretchedly at her hands clasped tightly in her lap. That's it then, she thought. I'm definitely not coming to see her again. If Letty goes on smuggling drink in to her, the hospital may move her to one of those places for that sort of problem. With any luck they might keep her out of circulation for months. Perhaps she won't live to come out at all, she thought, with a sudden pang of compassion as she glanced at Eleanor's face, drained now of anima-tion, not exactly tranquil but strangely vulnerable, lost.

But Eleanor, as though aware of Flora's covert scrutiny, suddenly grinned. 'Don't look so bloody miserable, Flora, you're a long time dead you know. My nanny used to say that; not, of course, in order to encourage the young to savour life while one has the chance. No, it was improving the shining hour, making the most of fleeting time: that was what she was on about – pious old boot! "Life is real, life is earnest and the grave is not its goal."' Eleanor's voice rang out as the door was opened by a nurse supporting an elderly, vacant-faced woman, whose tottering footsteps were being guided to the empty bed.

Hastily Flora stood up and leaned over Eleanor with some idea of muffling her voice with the baffle of her own body. But at sight of the nurse Eleanor had closed her eyes and fallen silent.

'I really must go now,' she said, but quietly in the hope that Eleanor really was about to fall asleep.

She heard herself saying, 'I don't know when I'll be able to visit you again, there's a lot to do before we go on holiday.'

Eleanor's eyelids flew up. 'You didn't tell me you were going away!'

'Well, we are.' Flora was making a great business of replacing her chair in the exact position in which she had found it. 'The change will do Fergus good.'

Eleanor raised her hand and gave her a brief insouciant wave. 'Byee,' she said.

116

All the way down the long, tiled corridor that smelt of shepherd's pie and disinfectant, Flora felt Eleanor's eyes following her, faintly hooded above the little amused smile.

The afternoon, spent in the grounds of the Grange, had also made its demands upon Fergus. But now, or so he thought, the worst was behind him.

He was relieved that Letty had not argued when he had suggested that he would sit in the sun instead of accompanying her to the kitchen. She could have pointed out that very little light, far less sun, filtered through the cedar branches to the peeling rustic bench under their shade. But Fergus had greeted its presence with unfeigned enthusiasm; if he'd had to walk another couple of yards he was convinced that his knees would have buckled under him.

He hastily stuffed his handkerchief, sweat-soaked from mopping his face, back into his pocket as he saw Letty returning across the lawn from the house. She was carrying a tall glass in each hand, and the expectation that the sight aroused lent genuine warmth to his smile.

Anticipation proved, not for the first time, to have been more pleasurable than ultimate gratification.

'Barley water and lemon. Home-made,' said Letty, as Fergus, after taking one eager sip, held the glass at almost arm's length and stared at its murky and definitely gin-less contents with an expression bordering on disbelief.

'First rate for the kidneys, y'know!'

Fergus nodded noncommitally; he preferred not to think about his kidneys or, for that matter, his liver.

'I couldn't have managed that job on my own. Horrid business. Hope it hasn't taken too much out of you?'

Fergus did his best to straighten up. 'No, no, I'm fine. Just fine! Perhaps not quite on top of my form, though. Still feeling the effects of the accident – surprising what a shock to the system that sort of thing can be.'

'I'll tell Eleanor when I see her this evening that we've attended to things. That'll put her mind at rest. Boots is missing her.' Letty nodded in the direction of the dog who was lying in the grass nearby, staring lugubriously into space. Fergus thought he looked much as usual.

'Poor Eleanor, she's always getting into some sort of pickle.' Letty slung her plump little legs up on to the seat, her muddied boots nearly touching Fergus's trousers. Fergus felt slightly ill at ease and it had nothing to do with the proximity of Letty's boots to his clothes, which were already so bespattered with soil and damp clay that a bit more mud would scarcely matter. No, what disturbed him was his suspicion that Letty might want to take advantage of Eleanor's absence to indulge in some sort of heart-to-heart chat. She kept herself, or was kept, very much in the background when Eleanor was present; so perhaps it was understandable that she should wish to seize the chance of enjoying his undivided attention.

'I do blame myself for having left Eleanor on her own, but it's not reasonable to expect me to be on duty, as it were, all the time – now, is it? Eleanor can be very trying.'

Fergus made disclamatory but vaguely sympathetic noises. His suspicions were being confirmed and it was obvious that it was about Eleanor that Letty wanted to talk. Tricky, that. He ought to make it clear that he had no intention of indulging in gossip about upstairs with downstairs! But the difficulty was that he had never been able to work out if Letty's relationship with Eleanor was basically that of an employee. On the other hand, if the relationship were not as clear-cut as that . . . well, Fergus felt no inhibitions about gossiping with and about equals. A little discretion was called for.

'I'm sure nobody, Eleanor least of all, could think that you don't take duty very seriously, my dear! Eleanor obviously thinks the world of you; nothing quite like old friends. You've known one another for years, haven't you? Perhaps I've got it wrong, but I gathered that you are also related?'

'I'm related to Alastair, actually. He's a sort of cousin. But not too close,' Letty added, not specifying for what purpose the relationship was sufficiently distant. 'You're right, we've known one another for years – for almost as long as I can remember, as a matter of fact. Grew up together in the same set. You know how it is. Eleanor was so beautiful – well, you can still tell. No other girl had a

119

look in while Eleanor was around, I can tell you! Alastair was *the* catch as far as our little crowd was concerned.' Letty stared into her glass. 'Anyway, they made what people call "a handsome couple", Alastair and Eleanor. Of course it couldn't last, I knew that; but then I know Eleanor! Poor Alastair felt very guilty about leaving her – still feels guilty, I suppose. Eleanor is good at making people feel guilty.'

Fergus felt increasingly uneasy. He wished Letty would hurry up and finish her foul drink so that he could take his leave.

'Rotten business when a marriage doesn't work out. But why did you think it wouldn't?'

'Eleanor has this thing, you see . . . she always ends up by destroying anyone who is really attracted to her. Sounds silly, I know, but it's not easy to explain it any other way.'

'Certainly doesn't make sense to me!'

'Then you'll just have to take my word for it. I've seen it happen time and time again, and not only before she and Alastair got married. Men used to be attracted to Eleanor like bees to a honey-pot – some still are.'

Fergus shifted himself a little on the bench; he could feel his shirt, still damp with sweat, sticking uncomfortably to his back.

'As I see it, Eleanor doesn't like herself very much, so she always develops a sort of contempt for anyone attracted to her. Not immediately, but after a time it always happens. Then she sets out to prove that they must be flawed too. She has an extraordinary instinct for detecting the weak spot, that flaw in the other person. She just rips them open and reveals themselves to themselves. People can't survive that, you know, having their self-respect torn away. But Eleanor just can't help it. Besides, it amuses her, she was always easily bored.'

Fergus attempted an avuncular little laugh. 'Oh now, surely you're letting your imagination run away with you, Letty! *You* stay with her – and you've said yourself that you've known one another since childhood. And you get along well, both of you – don't you?'

Letty was scraping with her fingernails at the dried mud on her dungarees, her face greenish in the light that struggled through the overhead branches.

'That's quite a different thing. I'm not attracted to Eleanor, not in love with her – not in that sense. Anyway, she needs me. She needs someone to confide in. She has no secrets from me, Fergus, I always know what Eleanor is up to. Besides,' she continued, not looking at him, intent apparently on a particularly stubborn stain, the scratching of her nails putting Fergus's teeth on edge, 'Besides, perhaps I don't have much self-respect that Eleanor can rob me of. You know, there is something to be said for remaining near the rich man's table; the crumbs do come one's way, after the loaves have been broken.'

Fergus heaved himself to his feet. 'A holiday! That's

what you need, Letty. You should take yourself off with Eleanor when she comes out of hospital. Do you both good.'

'No! What I need is a holiday from Eleanor!' Letty had scrambled to her feet and now placed a restraining hand on Fergus's arm. 'Don't go rushing off, Fergus. That's really what I wanted to talk to you about, my need for a little break. I'm writing to Alastair; I think he should get the hospital to persuade Eleanor to go into a convalescent home for a couple of weeks or so. There's a frightfully good place on the coast, run by nuns, actually. Eleanor went there once before – it's a sort of drying-out place; not that it'll achieve much with Eleanor in that direction, but it will take her off my hands for a little while.'

'Shouldn't think Eleanor would want to go – don't blame her either.'

'She'll go! Alastair is more generous to her than he need be, you see. But it does depend on her toeing the line. This drunken-driving affair will strengthen his hand. Ultimately Eleanor knows which side her bread is buttered.'

So do you, I bet, thought Fergus. He snapped his fingers at Boots. 'Come on, old chap – walkies down to the gate. I really must be off, Letty. You've obviously worked things out very well. It sounds fine. Eleanor will get really good attention and you'll get away for a holiday. Jolly good!'

122

Letty slipped her arm through his and kept pace with his lengthening stride as he walked rapidly across the lawn towards the drive. Boots gave up and dropped behind, collapsing again on the grass and mournfully resting his head between his paws.

Fergus did not stop until they reached the gate. Letty released her hold on his arm, but not before giving it a little squeeze.

'I'm so glad you approve, Fergus. I really do value your advice. It means such a lot – having someone to turn to. But I won't go away for my holiday. I'll stay here, there are the animals to think of, and other things.' She smiled up at him with what seemed to Fergus, for a fleeting moment, an unusually large number of strong little teeth.

Fergus was in the kitchen when Flora returned, slumped at the table, a pot of tea at his elbow.

'I've just brewed it, if you want a cup,' he said as she banged her bag and gloves down on the table. 'How is she?' he asked, not seeming to notice how roughly Flora had thrust her cup towards him.

'One arm in plaster, some sort of head injury, but otherwise very much as usual. Which may or may not be anything to worry about.'

'Good, good,' said Fergus, abstractedly.

Flora looked at him sharply. His face was pale with fatigue and she saw, with growing irritation, that his pullover was earth-stained, the collar of his shirt crumpled, and his wellington boots, covered in mud, were still on his outstretched feet. Only guilt, she thought, could have driven him to such a sudden excess of zealous gardening.

'What have you been up to? You won't do yourself any good by going at the garden like a bull at a gate. It's not even as though you're used to it.'

'I wouldn't exactly call it gardening!' Fergus was removing his wellingtons, easing them off against the table leg as though too weary to bend down.

'What have you been up to, then?'

'If you must know, I've been giving Letty a hand, burying Nicholas Nye. My God, I wish I could get my hands on the louts who did him in! The wound in his throat looked as though it had been made with a crossbow, but not content with that they'd hacked him about, mutilated the poor old fellow. Ghastly business!'

'You mean . . . when did it happen?'

'Tuesday night!' Fergus looked surprised at Flora's evident bewilderment. 'Surely I told you?'

Flora shook her head.

'I only heard about it on Wednesday night . . . with everything else that happened then, it must have slipped my mind. I was sure I told you . . .' Fergus paused, he recalled that he had been too drunk on Wednesday night for him to remember what he had told, or failed to tell Flora. 'When Eleanor told me, I thought he'd been killed outright. It wasn't until I saw him that I realised just

124

what a horrible job they'd made of it. No wonder she got . . . well, drank a bit more than was wise! But she just kept crying about him having been killed, so I didn't get a very clear picture of just how awful it had been, if you see what I mean. They must be subhuman, people who could do a thing like that. He never did them any harm . . . poor stupid old thing.'

'Nicholas Nye! Yes, of course, I see now!'

'Didn't Eleanor tell you about it?'

'Well, she said something but I wasn't very clear about what she meant – but she was distressed, so I didn't press her. It happened on Tuesday night, you said?'

'Then, or perhaps early on the Wednesday morning. Eleanor found him when she went out to see him after breakfast. That's what started her on a binge. By evening she was in a pretty bad way and there was no drink left in the house – I told you that she went to the pub to get a bottle. That's when I met her.'

'But how hadn't she heard anything, I mean, he must have . . .' Flora suddenly remembered that she had heard Nicholas Nye; heard him as she had sewed in the kitchen.

'She'd had a few over the top before she went to bed on Tuesday. Got a bit sozzled. I expect she'd have been deaf to the last trump. Letty should never have left her alone; she blames herself for that.'

Flora looked down at her hands and started to push down the cuticles of her thumbnails with dedicated concentration.

'She says there must have been some sort of mis-understanding when she rang you on Sunday. Told me to tell you not to blame yourself; easy to get things wrong on the bally phone, of course.'

Flora cleared the cups from the table and took them to the sink and called out to Fergus from the scullery.

'You'd better get out of those clothes; have a good hot bath.'

But he was still sitting where she had left him when she returned to the kitchen, staring bleakly at the marigolds in their jug, the flowers as jaunty as when they'd been plucked for Stella's pleasure.

'I've had a ghastly afternoon, Flora. You've no idea! And burying Nicholas Nye, that was one helluva job. The poor old chap had dragged himself up towards the house, there was a trail of blood on the grass . . . he got as far as the shrubbery. That made things a bit easier, for burying him, I mean. The ground there's pretty loamy so we dug a hole more or less where he fell. Got a rope round his legs and hauled him down over the edge of the hole.'

Flora put her hands over her ears.

'We didn't manage to dig as deep as we'd have liked. Struck clay y'know. But we finished it off with a sort of cairn of stones from the rockery; that should stop any foxes from grubbing around. Poor old Nicholas Nye!'

He rose stiffly, supporting his weight on his hands, splayed on the table, his nails black-edged with soil. His thick woollen stockings which had worked forward when he'd pulled off his wellingtons now flapped several inches beyond his toes like grey flippers.

Flora found herself at his side, her arm round his shoulders.

'He'd had a good innings, poor old fellow. I know it must have been horrific, seeing him like that, but he was probably dead in minutes. I expect he never really knew what was happening.'

'I know, I know. Just a donkey pottering about in a quiet field, not amounting to much, one way or another!'

'I didn't say that.'

'No, you didn't say it, but that's what you're thinking. What was it that Stella said about my fish – "when all's said and done, it's only a matter of a few ruddy fish".'

Flora let her arm drop.

'Now you're being ridiculous.'

'Ridiculous! Yes, that's a good word. I am, you know, I am – I'm not arguing with you.'

'Fergus! I refuse to be inveigled into silly bickering. It's all too . . .' Flora hesitated, seeking an alternative for 'ridiculous', 'unreasonable for words. I've had a hellish afternoon listening to Eleanor's nonsense; flippant one minute, self-pitying the next. If you ask me, she should never have been entrusted with looking after anything as innocent as a donkey. But I know you've had a trying few days – now just have your bath, a stiff drink and then, for God's sake, snap out of it.'

Fergus took a deep breath and then, suddenly, let it out, wordlessly.

I should have spoken to him like this years ago, thought Flora, as his ribcage and belligerence collapsed before her eyes.

'Oh – before I forget, Eleanor was very particular that I tell you that she's sticking to her guns; whatever that may mean!'

Fergus made no reply, just shifted his gaze so that it rested on the door jamb.

'What do you suppose she meant by that?'

'Ah . . . something to do with the accident, I expect. Yes, that would be it. She told the police that the fellow on the bike swerved out in front of the car and I expect he denies it.'

Flora knew he was lying. Intuitively she felt that the truth, like the sleeping dog, ought to be left undisturbed.

Flora had a sure and delicate touch with soufflés, a small accomplishment in which she took a modest pride. In the past, a succession of recuperating boys in the San at Windy Ridge had been nourished on what she regarded as the ideal panacea, whose meticulous preparation implied loving concern and whose consistency cosseted the digestion and coaxed the wayward appetite.

Now, as she deftly folded the foam of whipped egg white into the creamy cheese base, Flora's mind was occupied not with memories of Matron's cramped diet kitchen, but with more immediate considerations. Somehow or other she must work Fergus round to the idea of taking a holiday. A vague acceptance of the desirability of taking a holiday at some unspecified time in the future would not be enough; but if Fergus ran true to form it was probably as much as he was likely to concede. She must get him to agree, at least in principle, that they should go on holiday very soon because if, before being primed, he were to learn that she had already told Eleanor that they were going away, he would set himself absolutely against any such idea. Perhaps because Fergus so rarely made any decisions it was important for him to believe that such as were taken were entirely of his making. Why does everything have to be so difficult? Flora wondered with a sudden spurt of exasperation. Nothing, but nothing, ever seems to be straightforward, uncomplicated.

I'll just have to play it by ear, she decided, tenderly consigning the dish to the oven. It's greatly a matter of timing, she reminded herself, glancing at her watch and calculating how long it would be before the soufflé would be ready to serve. I will not attempt to broach the subject until Fergus has been fed; wined too, she decided, remembering the solitary bottle which she had bought to replace the one that Stella had so casually taken from the sideboard. If Fergus demurred about the wine, then she could say 'why shouldn't we indulge ourselves a little?' – that would make an excellent opening gambit to discussing the possibility of other little treats which they might allow themselves. I must remember not to take the opportunity to point out that while he considers the occasional bottle of wine an exorbitant extravagance, his own whisky and Eleanor's gin are never considered to be unnecessary luxuries.

In the event, it was Fergus who introduced the subject which was uppermost in Flora's mind.

'Do you know what we are going to do, Flora?' he asked, scraping the last of the cheese soufflé from the sides of the dish. 'We're going on holiday!'

To strengthen this unexpected resolve, Flora offered objections to his suggestion, but they were carefully selected as being of a type which could readily be countered.

'But it's so late in the year, Fergus! I mean, the beginning of October isn't exactly the best time, surely?'

'A bit late, perhaps – but that's all the more reason to get away as soon as we can. It'll set us up for the winter.'

'But the garden . . .'

'Oh, that'll still be there when we get back.'

That, thought Flora, was only too true. Any previous attempts on her part to get away had been dismissed by Fergus either on the grounds that the care of his fish could not be entrusted to anyone else or that money was too tight. The second of these objections probably held good, so Flora did not risk raising it. She ought to have felt relieved by his sudden determination.

Flora glanced covertly at Fergus. He was pink and fresh after his bath, his newly washed hair silken and silver as thistledown. Snuggled into his old paisley dressing gown he resembled a child who had been granted the treat of eating late supper like the grown-ups.

'Well, what d'you think?' His bluffness sounded contrived.

'What sort of holiday have you in mind – France, Austria?'

It would be a pleasant change to go abroad untrammelled by the presence of small boys with their tendency to develop measles, to run temperatures, to attract the attention of stinging insects and to fall victim to attacks of diarrhoea.

Fergus shook his head. 'Neither. Tangie Bay – that's what I have in mind! A couple of weeks or so at the dear old Golf View . . . a walk down memory lane, eh?' He gave a little self-conscious laugh.

Discomfited, Flora glanced away. The curtains were undrawn and in the window, against the darkling garden, the image of Fergus was reflected back at her like a doppelgänger.

'Should be quite reasonable,' he went on, as though eager to press the practical advantages. 'Off-season rates at this time of year, I shouldn't wonder. We could go up by train to save that long drive which I wouldn't fancy. No trippers cluttering up the place. Breath of sea air . . .' His hands were restless, busying themselves aligning and realigning his table-mat, the cutlery on his plate, his wine glass.

'Tangie! Yes, Fergus, why not?' Yes, indeed, why not – so how could she account for this frisson of unease? Dismissing it, Flora smiled brightly across the table at Fergus. 'I'll bring the coffee into the sitting room and we can get down to making plans. Or perhaps you'd rather leave the details until later, when you'll be more rested?'

'No, no! Why hang about?' Fergus had risen and, to Flora's surprise, started to help her clear the table.

'I'll phone the hotel in the morning. I thought we might take the night-train tomorrow; there shouldn't be any difficulty getting sleepers at this time of year.'

But the packing! thought Flora; the suitcases buried under God knows what in the boxroom . . . and there's the milkman, the papers . . . and my most comfortable shoes still at the menders.

'Oh yes, I expect we can manage quite easily,' she said with a commendable air of brisk confidence.

First thing in the morning, she thought, I can wash the pullovers we'll certainly need to take with us. Please don't let it rain. Of course by morning Fergus may have changed his mind – that would be just like him! But as he is behaving so uncharacteristically, I can't even predict what he may, or may not, do next.

8
~

Flora stood in the lee of a ramshackle refreshment kiosk
which had already been boarded up in readiness for the
storms of winter. Her back to the desolate harbour and
the gusting east wind, she looked with deliberate detachment at the rash of bathing huts that fringed the beach,
and the garish glitter of caravans which cluttered the
expanse of green where once the fishing nets had been
spread to dry. It doesn't matter, she told herself, none of
this has anything to do with me.

She felt heavy from lack of sleep. During the night-
long journey she had lain tense in her bunk, overtired by
the frantic rush of preparation, unable to allow her body
to relax with the movement of the train. The seeds of
doubt in her mind as to the advisability of returning to
Tangie Bay had germinated in the stuffy darkness, had
sprouted and spread their pallid tentacles until there was

133

no room left in her head for anything but the consideration of the folly of Fergus's sudden decision.

But the injunction that had plagued her throughout the
night – that one should never go back to a place where
one had known happiness – now seemed to make less
sense. The Tangie Bay which she had known was particular to herself, and the memory of it, imprinted on her
mind, was not subject to change, was inviolate. To return
to it was obviously a physical impossibility so its reality
for her could in no way be threatened by this visit to a
particular geographical location.

A little apart from the village, on its knoll to the south
of what was now the caravan park, Peepie Cottage still
stood. It looked unchanged, exposed to the wind, its windows looking seaward, the little skylight set in the
blue-grey slates glinting like ice. She remembered running
to the village early in the mornings to fetch the breakfast
baps and butteries from the bakery in Harbour Street.
String bag dangling from one hand, a florin clutched in
the other; the dew on the grass soaking her sandshoes, the
air full of the cries of the gulls swooping over the harbour
and filled with the smell of tar, seaweed and golden whin.
There must have been mornings when it had rained, but
these memory had wiped from the slate of remembrance.

She happed her coat more tightly around her, buried
her chin deep in its collar, and began the walk up the village main thoroughfare which rose, steep and straight as
a die, before her. Here things were apparently little

changed. The doors of the houses opened directly on to the pavement; the small windows, deep-set in the grey stone walls, peered out at the legs of the passers-by – and there were few of those on this chill October afternoon. She was not tempted, as she had been on her outward walk, to turn off into the narrow lanes that opened off the cobbled street; even the shelter they offered from the wind did not compensate for the visible changes which had challenged her resolve not to be dismayed by evidence of loss of what had been.

She hurried past the church and its surrounding graveyard; its low encircling wall was no longer topped with the rusted spears of the iron railings which had enclosed it in the past. They must have been removed for scrap during the war and never replaced, she thought, averting her gaze from the huddle of round-shouldered gravestones that rose above the salt-bleached grass and leaned together in grey and silent communion.

Flora had left Fergus stretched out on his bed surrounded by the contents of his partially unpacked suitcase, and had fully expected to find him in the same position on her return. To her surprise, she found him sitting in the hotel lounge gazing unenthusiastically at the afternoon tea set before him.

'There used to be sandwiches and chocolate cake, now look at it!' he complained in lieu of greeting, and jabbing a finger in the direction of a plate of soggy buttered toast and a couple of foil-wrapped biscuits.

Flora threw her coat over the back of a chair and sank down on to its tired springs.

'That was over forty years ago, Fergus. Things change.' She caught the eye of the elderly waitress who brought a second cup and rearranged the tea service so that the handles of both teapot and hot water jug faced Flora.

'Much changed in the village, then?'

Flora struggled forward in her chair. 'The sort of thing one would expect – bathing huts, caravans. Most of the small shops in Harbour Street have gone, including that lovely old bakery. But there's a self-service store and a vulgar little souvenir shop which is shut up for the season. Half the old cottages in the lanes seem to be empty, I expect they're only holiday homes now. And the lanes themselves, they've been properly made up – for cars, I suppose. No more mussel shells!' Briefly she saw again the remembered blue-black and milky grey surface that had crackled and crunched under one's sandalled feet.

'Used to stink to high heaven on hot days,' said Fergus. 'No need for mussel-bait these days. The woman at the desk was telling me that there's no fishing from here now – bloody Common Market put the kibosh on that. There's a bit of lobster fishing still and the tourists bring in some money. But the old life's gone, finished.' He stared gloomily about him, a smear of butter glistening on his chin.

136

'What was it that you expected to find, Fergus?'

But if he knew, then he wasn't telling.

'See that fellow over there – the skinny chap by the window?' He had lowered his voice to what he imagined was a confidential pitch. 'Syme's his name. Goes for a swim before breakfast every morning. Imagine, in this weather! Bloody fool.'

'Oh I don't know. If he enjoys it, why not?'

'Jogging down Harbour Street in a track suit, just a show-off, if you ask me.'

'Does he play golf?'

'How should I know?'

'No reason. I just thought that if you'd been speaking to him . . .'

'I told you, it was that woman in Reception, Mrs Lindsay, I think she's the manageress. Anyway, I had a bit of a chat with her. She remembers you, by the way.'

Flora was surprised at the pleasure she felt in hearing that someone in Tangie Bay should remember her, and yet the pleasure was tinged with an indefinable sense of dismay that there was someone here who might embark on the 'do you remember' game and force upon her the realisation that there was now more to remember than to look forward to.

She frowned suddenly. 'But I was only seventeen the last time I was here, I can't possibly look anything like I did then. Even my name is changed.'

'Well, I told you we got talking. As soon as I told her

137

that your family used to come here and that you stayed at Peepie Cottage, she placed you right away. She'd be about your age, I think. It was her aunt who owned Peepie Cottage – funny coincidence, what!'

Coincidences made Flora uneasy, but just why that should be so she would have found difficult to explain, even to herself. She did suspect that that unease was occasioned by the notion of 'the long arm' of coincidence . . . a long arm stretching out, manipulating at will.

Flora shook her head. 'Can't say that I remember. But now that I come to think of it, there was a girl who sometimes gave Mrs Davidson a hand with the washing-up and so forth.'

Memory teased her with a fleeting glimpse, hazy as an old snapshot, of a girl being one of a group of women seated round the kitchen table at Peepie Cottage.

'Married when she was very young, during the war. He was in a minesweeper. Drowned at sea, poor fellow.'

Flora said nothing. She did not share Fergus's interest in other peoples tragedies, failures or shortcomings.

He jerked his head in the direction of the small group of guests who sat in armchairs ranged round the fire.

'That lot are regulars. They hole up here for the winter. They start arriving at the close of the season and leave before Easter.'

He made them sound like migratory birds, thought Flora, casting an eye in their direction. Yes, a brace of plump partridges; a fish-hawk, eyes sunken now with age but the overall expression still predatory; a clutch of twittering dunnets showing signs of moult. Where did they fly to when Easter came – a perch under the roof of a dutiful relative? Or perhaps their own homes awaited them, damp from disuse, leaves in the gutters and dead flies on the windowsills.

'Not a bad idea, once one is getting on a bit. They get special reduced rates, you see.' Fergus sounded reflective.

Flora stood up. 'Fergus . . .' and hesitated. What she wanted to say must wait until later when she might be better able to withstand argument. 'I think I'll go upstairs. There's time for a bath before dinner.'

She'd change into the dress Stella had sent her. A chic, extravagant creation and utterly unsuitable for the dismal ambience of The Golf View.

Tomorrow, she promised herself, climbing the stairs, holding herself very straight and resolutely refusing to as much as touch the bannister rail, tomorrow we will move away to some place that holds neither memory of youth past nor portent of what might yet be to come.

But in the morning the sun shone, the wind had dropped to no more than a light-hearted breeze and the herring gulls swooped and cried in a pellucid sky.

'It's a late Indian Summer,' the residents twittered, having perhaps long abandoned hope that there could be such a thing. Mr Syme, his hair plastered damply to his skull, looked up briefly from his prunes and bran to nod agreement, but with the rather superior air proper to one to whom sun or shower were of little consequence.

After breakfast Fergus took himself and Flora out on to the golf course. Perhaps all I needed was a decent night's sleep, Flora thought, feeling her spirits rising in air that was cool without being unpleasantly so and which was charged with a smell of the sea. For his part, Fergus was more cheerful than she could recall him having been for some time. Even when his ball landed in the wicked bunker below the fourth green, his good humour was not quenched.

'Just like old times!' he shouted up at her, his shoes half buried in the soft sand.

He spent some time in the bunker, but when at last the ball was persuaded to trickle a few yards beyond its lip, Fergus scrambled back on to the fairway with his temper unimpaired. Things might have been different if there had been witnesses to his floundering efforts but, the summer being deemed to be over, the players had departed and they had the course to themselves.

Halfway round, his energies beginning to flag, Fergus suggested that the time had come to take a breather. They made for the nearby headland, wading through the heather, its spent brown blossom rustling to the ground in their wake. A flurry of grouse rose from almost under their feet, crying in alarm 'goback, goback', as they whirred away low over the moorland.

Together they sat on a lichened boulder and looked

down at the familiar cove below them. Fergus put his arm round Flora's shoulders, but as the boulder was barely wide enough to accommodate both of them, she could not be sure if the gesture was born of affection or a need for balance.

'Hasn't changed all that!' he said, turning his head in the direction of the village. From where they sat, the village appeared as no more than an irrelevant huddle of grey stone, its bathing huts and caravans mere specks on the landscape. It was the sea itself that dominated, flooded the eye with its grey-blue immensity.

Today, with only the lightest of breezes to ruffle its surface, it was a gentle sea that glinted in the pale sunshine. The dance of its waves was demure, the foam on their caps no more than a modest frosting of lace. Only the outgoing tide did not hide its strength as it pulled the waves steadily ever further back from each playful run at the shore. Flora could hear the sea breathing – in, out, in, out, as though it dozed in the last of the summer's sun.

'I used to sit here sometimes, watching you and your aunts and mother down there in the cove.'

'I never knew that!'

'Well, I did.'

Oh what bliss that knowledge would once have brought her! Flora looked back with wry wonder at that period of agonised adolescent yearning when she had both craved and feared the slightest acknowledgement from Fergus that she even existed. Oh the pain of that infatuation and her anxiety to conceal it! It was unlikely that she had succeeded in deceiving anyone with, of course, the exception of Fergus himself. People thought that young love was comical; endearing perhaps, but definitely daft. But Flora remembered it as having been akin to an all-absorbing illness. There had been the confused sense of shame, too, that she should harbour such painful longing for a young man whom she did not, in any real sense, know at all. Thank God, she thought, that I can never be seventeen again.

Flora laughed as a more manageable memory came to her.

'Do you remember your mother's sealyhams?'

'Tansy and Trudi? Can't say I thought they were funny – yapping little nuisances!'

'Oh but they were funny, Fergus! I'll never forget their little chamois leather boots.'

'Could anyone forget those ridiculous boots? The hours I spent searching for them when they lost them! Without them, Mother was convinced that the sand would irritate their paws and they'd get sores between their pads. More trouble than they were worth, that pair.'

'I thought those boots were a great idea.'

'You did? Made us a laughing-stock – those crazy boots.'

Had Fergus really thought it had been just a matter of chance that she had so often appeared on the scene when he was searching the dunes for missing canine footwear?

Scarcely a word or a look exchanged between them; in the distance her mother keeping a watchful eye, an eye that had been keen enough to have spotted the searching Fergus in the first place. 'There's that nice Sinclair boy hunting the slipper again. You'd better run along and lend him a hand, Flora.' Oh, the humiliation of that complicity!

But on the day of the storm it had been Bruce, not Fergus, who had been left behind to search the dunes. Mrs Munro had not accompanied the aunts and Flora on that afternoon walk and, even if she had been with them, she would have been unlikely to have sent Flora off in aid of Bruce. Mrs Munro's ambitions had had their bounds and, early on in her match-making campaign, she had accepted that Bruce was off-limits. Fergus, she had shrewdly reasoned, would constitute almost as good 'a catch' for her daughter as Bruce; but by virtue of being the younger son might be landed with less parental opposition.

All that morning they'd been cooped up in Peepie Cottage while the gale had dashed the rain against the windows, rattled the doors and gusted down the chimney sending soot pattering on to the hearth. By the time lunch was over, the air had been heavy with animosity, the tension between the aunts and Mrs Munro having mounted as the barometer fell. When Aunt Agnes had declared that the rain had almost spent itself and she intended going for a walk, Flora and Annie had hastened to button themselves into their raincoats and, their berets jammed well down over their ears, had thankfully gone with her.

Flora was quite startled to hear Fergus's voice at her side.

'Think I'll stretch out for a few minutes – make the most of the sun.' He'd lifted his arm from her shoulders, was spreading his anorak on the ground. Flora could see the bulge of the whisky flask in his pocket and guessed that he was impatient for the opportunity of a quick and private nip.

Perversely, she waited for him to suggest that she take a walk before she rose to saunter along the cliff top. The ground sloped steadily downwards and soon the Daisy Rock was clearly visible, its spine extending into the sea like a natural jetty; it marked the end of the dunes that lay between it and the village and the beginning of the rising heather moor.

Today it looked so calm, so benign, that Flora thought the rock resembled some huge primeval lizard napping in the sun. It was not easy to reconcile its present appearance with the terrifying aspect it had presented on the day that had forced an intimacy between the Sinclairs and the Munros.

On that day the waves had crashed with such ferocious force against the beach that even on the path between the dunes Flora and her aunts had been drenched by the spume that had been flung over them in short, fierce flurries. Flora, having sighted Bruce searching in the dunes, was on the alert for a glimpse of Fergus and she was the first to see not only Fergus but Mrs Sinclair and young Stella standing on the landward side of the Daisy Rock.

Flora had tugged at Aunt Agnes's sleeve to draw her attention to the unexpected sight of the rarefied Mrs Sinclair abroad on such a day. One sealyham dangled awkwardly under Fergus's arm and suddenly the other dog rushed forward along the rock with Stella close behind it in pursuit. Both disappeared from sight down the far side of the ridge, but soon the dog was visible again through a haze of flying foam, rushing back to his mistress who had seemingly gone mad. Mrs Sinclair was jumping up and down, waving desperately in their direction, her long scarf, held high above her head, streaming out in the wind.

Only seconds had passed since Flora had directed Agnes's attention towards the Daisy Rock, but before Flora had grasped the significance of Mrs Sinclair's frenzied capering, Agnes was pounding along the path.

Vividly, Flora remembered the sick horror of the realisation, as she raced behind her aunt, that now Mrs Sinclair stood alone on the ridge, alone except for the sealyhams leaping excitedly round her legs.

Agnes well in the lead, Flora and Annie following her, they had raced past Mrs Sinclair, who seemed not to notice their arrival so intent was she on screaming for

Bruce, her voice as thin as the call of a curlew on the gale that tossed it away. Along the exposed ridge of the Daisy Rock they ran and then scrambled as far down its rocky side as the grasping waves would allow. Clinging to one another, their senses numbed by the scouring wind, they had watched Fergus's struggle to bring himself and Stella out of the water.

Twice, in an agony of impotence, they saw him flung clear of the waves almost upon the rocks and twice the sea snatched him back. It seemed to play with him like an angler with a fish on the line; and, like a hooked fish, Fergus was tiring.

Flora, unable to bear to watch any longer, had screwed her eyes tight shut and prayed. How she had prayed! Her eyes were still closed when Fergus made his third and ultimately successful attempt to snatch a handhold on a tangle of kelp that clung like the roots of a tree from a fissure in the rocks below them.

Agnes flung herself flat on the rocks and, with Annie and Flora gripping her ankles, she managed to get a firm hold on Stella, enabling Fergus to use both his hands to haul himself to safety.

It had been the very stuff of melodrama! When Fergus had leaned his weight on Flora and spewed water all over her already sodden feet, she had been so overcome by the sheer romance of it all that she had come close to emulating the faint which had already laid Mrs Sinclair low.

But the stillness of Stella, spread-eagled on the short turf of the Daisy Rock a few yards away from her prostrate mother, was of a different and more frightening sort. Her clothes too water-logged and her hair too sodden to be stirred by the gale, she was the only thing on the Daisy Rock that was utterly motionless.

Undaunted, Agnes had set to work.

'A miracle!' Annie had shouted when the child began to breathe and stir.

'Nonsense!' was Agnes's curt reply. ' "The Lord helps those who help themselves." '

In the days that followed, Agnes had regarded with a lofty amusement Flora's mother's assiduous efforts to observe that very maxim. Both Stella and Fergus might have died on the Daisy Rock that day had not the Munro women been there and Mrs Sinclair must be made to realise that a bond now existed between the two families – a bond which Mrs Munro was determined to exploit to full advantage.

Mrs Sinclair, having declared that she was suffering from both chill and shock, took to her bed for several days. There she might have remained for an even longer period had it not been for Mrs Munro's persistence in visiting her bearing gifts of Brands' Essence and tonic wine.

Stella's discharge from the cottage hospital was celebrated by a treat in the form of a visit to the circus which was making its annual visit to Kirktown. Flora's delight at being invited to join the party was only slightly tempered by the spectacle of her mother's all too evident satisfaction.

The link that had been forged that afternoon on the Daisy Rock held even when Fergus returned to university in the Autumn.

How careless one was with time when one was young, thought Flora, remembering how she had been forever wishing it to hurry along; impatient for schooldays to be over, longing to be 'grown-up', to fall in love, to get married, to have a family of her own. Forever straining forward and neglecting to savour the present. Whole chunks of time squandered in a fever of anticipation.

But, although it had seemed as though it never would, August had come again and the Munros were back in Peepie Cottage and the Sinclairs once more installed in The Golf View. That had been the summer of 1939 and the last that any of them would spend together in Tangie Bay. Flora could not recall that the prospect of war had dampened their spirits; if anything, it had given a sense of urgency, an added excitement, to her own and Fergus's determination to extract the last ounce of enjoyment from that holiday. Oh the mooning and the spooning, the protestations of eternal love . . .

Well, Flora told herself brusquely as she turned her back on the Daisy Rock and began the climb up to the golf course, only a moonstruck calf would be foolish enough to expect that sort of infatuation to last forever. If life . . . if Fergus . . . had not fulfilled her expectations, then all she could do was to accept the fact. Hard cheese! Even the sweetest of cream could turn into that – given time.

I'll send a postcard to Eleanor. One of those romantic views of the harbour at sunset. 'Wonderful weather – we're enjoying a real Indian Summer!' No, she'd address it to Letty and add, 'Hope Eleanor is behaving herself!' which would put Eleanor in her place as of being of no more consequence than a tiresome child.

Fergus was where she had left him, but standing now, staring out over the sea, a solitary figure in that treeless windswept expanse. She called out to him, but he did not turn his head until she had almost reached his side and then he looked surprised to see her.

'Penny for them?' asked Flora, taking refuge in the childish phrase to mask the real concern she felt at the sight of Fergus's lost and distracted expression.

'Penny for what?'

'Your thoughts of course, silly! You looked miles away.' Why do I have to sound so flippant, why can't I say, Darling, tell me what is bothering you? According to popular belief, she shouldn't even have to ask. Old married couples were reputed to know instinctively what was going on in one another's heads – My God, perhaps it was as well that that was probably nothing but a myth.

'As a matter of fact, I was thinking about my aquarium. Well, in a way that was what I was thinking about.'

'You will restock it, won't you Fergus? It'll be rather fun starting it up again from scratch.' I must encourage him, saucers of worms on the draining board notwithstanding. Whatever would he fill his time with if he didn't have his wretched fish to fuss over?

'Thinking about the way they died – all of them.'

'Oh Fergus, no good brooding over that. These things do happen, one just has to put that sort of thing behind one. Of course it was awful, but the thing now is to plan the restocking.' He's not even listening, I might as well save my breath to cool my porridge as Aunt Agnes used to say.

'You see, fish that seem to be perfectly healthy are, in fact, generally harbouring disease. But it lies dormant, may never surface at all. So one goes on thinking everything is fine. Deluding oneself. But then something activates the hidden sickness. It could be stress, chill . . . or the introduction of an outsider which is actively ill. Do you understand? It's there all the time. It's just an illusion that there isn't a flaw – do you see?'

'Surely it's the same with human beings? Don't we carry germs all the time but only succumb to them under certain circumstances?'

'Exactly! One is unaware . . . and then something or someone triggers it off, and wham!'

'So you realise now that the Rose Clown was only the catalyst? Anything might have set them off – is that what you are saying?'

Fergus bent down and picked up his clubs. 'Yes, a cat-alyst, that's all it needs.'

'Well, I'm glad you've come round to seeing it like that. After all, how could Stella have been expected to foresee the effect her action would have? I think you should write to her, explain. I know it was understandable at the time – the way you flew off the handle – but you obviously upset her. Yes, I do think you should write her a nice letter. She'd appreciate that.'

'Who would?'

'Stella, of course! Fergus, have you listened to a word I've said?'

'Oh yes. Write a letter to Stella, that's what you said.'

Flora slipped her arm under his. 'Come on, better finish the round. There's still time.'

9

~

Flora showed no signs of being tearful and that, thought Stella, was something for which she was thankful.

Stella had not looked forward to the probability of having to deal with tears. She considered weeping to be a messy and embarrassing activity and one which, if it must be practised, should be indulged only in private.

But although Flora was not crying, she did look disorientated, somewhat dazed. She stood in the centre of the large, airy bedroom wearing the air of a traveller who had found herself lost in a square in some strange city and who stood there bemused, uncertain as to which road had led her there and puzzled as to which would take her back to familiar territory.

'I felt awful about you being left on your own here for so long. But you do understand, don't you, why I didn't get here any earlier?'

'Oh yes. The woman I spoke to in your London

office – I think she's your secretary – she explained that they were having difficulty in contacting you. She wasn't even sure if you were still in Switzerland. You were taking a little holiday, she said, after the business part of your trip was over.'

'That's right! The thing was, you see, that I'd arranged to phone in from time to time and, as luck would have it, I'd rung only a few hours before they heard from you. Everything was running smoothly so I didn't bother to get in touch again for a week. I think it's good for them to have to cope without me every now and again. After all, no one's indispensable, as they say. One never knows what may happen to one from one day to the next.'

'That's so true.' Flora smiled, a little bleakly. 'But thanks for coming so quickly after you did hear what had happened. You must be worn out after such a dash.'

'Oh I'm fine!' Stella tossed a very new-looking black felt hat on to one of the beds and ran her fingers through her hair. Her suit, too, was black: barathea, elegant but understated. She has obviously, thought Flora, come prepared . . .

'Actually, it's over. It was the day before yesterday, the . . .' she hesitated, 'cremation' sounded, paradoxically, so cold, '. . . the funeral. Mrs Lindsay, the manageress, she sort of took charge of things for me. She thought it would be best to go ahead and get it over with. We didn't know how long it might be before you heard. I'm sorry we didn't wait, Stella, but I'm sure you understand.'

I must be sounding so wooden, thought Flora, but that's how I feel. Everything will be all right once Stella comes, I kept telling myself, but now that she is here I feel as though I'm imprisoned in a glass box and she's outside. Perhaps if I could reach out, touch her—

'Of course I understand, dear, you did the right thing. But what I don't understand is why you stayed on here after . . . well, it couldn't have been easy for you.'

'I had to really. For one thing there was the inquest, you see. And then it just seemed best to . . . well, to finish with it all here in Tangie Bay. Everyone has been so good to me, Stella. So kind! Mrs Lindsay has been simply wonderful.' Flora had sat down in one of the two armchairs by the window.

'The residents all came to the . . . the service . . . it was just as though they'd really known Fergus, both of us. Of course most of them are rather elderly so I expect they've got in quite a bit of practice for that sort of thing over the years!' I'm just havering on. Whoever heard of anyone being described as 'an awfully good chap at a funeral' in the way one said 'he's wonderful at a party'?

Oh heavens! Now she is going to cry, thought Stella, observing the sudden dip of Flora's head, the way her fingers fumbled with the buttons of her cardigan. To her relief, Flora lifted her head, looked quite composed again.

'Everything was done very nicely. Mrs Lindsay laid on sherry, sandwiches, that sort of thing, for when we all got back here . . .' In fact, thought Flora, her voice trailing away, it had all turned into a strange sort of little party, but decorous. Hard to tell just when it had changed from solemnity into more of a celebration of the circumstance of being still alive. Perhaps the start of the change had been when old Mrs Anderson had slipped from playing 'Abide with Me' on the piano into 'Roses of Picardy'; but she had played some twiddly little bits in between so that the transition had sounded quite natural. Flora hadn't heard 'Shine on Harvest Moon' since she'd been a child, and then it had been on the old wind-up gramophone. Flora smiled.

Stella relaxed, took out her cigarettes. Flora, her movements more supple now, fetched an ashtray from the dressing table.

'I didn't think of asking for a separate room for you – do you mind sharing?'

''Course not! In any case, it's only for tonight. I think I – both of us, really – ought to get back tomorrow. There's an afternoon plane.'

'We came up by train – overnight, you know. I've still got the return halves of the tickets. Fergus had forgotten to put his wallet in his pocket; so they're still there, the tickets and so forth, all safe and sound. Home and dry, you might say.' Flora turned and looked at the door. 'Mrs Lindsay said she'd bring us up some tea, she thought we'd prefer to be private. You must be longing for something.'

'We can have something stronger than tea to be getting

on with!' Stella was on her feet, unzipping her overnight bag, taking out her travelling flask.

Flora watched as she poured a generous dram into each of the tooth-glasses from the shelf above the wash-basin. It seemed such a long time ago when last she'd watched Stella do much the same thing in the bedroom at Hillcrest; but really it was no time at all. Stella was real again, familiar.

'Stella!' she said in a rush. 'You don't know how wonderful it is to have you here. I've just been waiting here in a strange sort of limbo. I almost began to think that nothing was *real*, not even myself. Oh, I can't explain . . . but, God, am I glad to see you!'

Stella's hand rested briefly on her shoulder as she placed the glass in Flora's outstretched hand.

'You get this down you and then tell me exactly what happened. The message I got had only the barest of details you know. Poor old Fergus, I still find it difficult to believe . . .'

'It was an accident. The coroner said so.'

'You were there – when it happened, I mean?'

'Oh no!' How strange that Stella should have to ask that. But, of course, of all the people under the roof of The Golf View, Stella must be the only one who knew practically nothing of the circumstances of her own brother's death.

With Stella sitting opposite her, so very attentive and so unusually grave-faced, Flora felt as though she were

making a formal report. She folded her hands in front of
her on the little table, fixed her eyes on the window
where the rain coursed like tears down the glass, and
began to relate the sequence of relevant events as clearly
as she could.

'We'd only been here a couple of days. Then I wak-
ened early one morning, I think it was the sound of the
door closing behind Fergus that disturbed me, and I saw
that he wasn't in his bed. I drifted off to sleep again.
Later, when I woke up properly, I saw that his bed was
still empty and there was a scrap of paper propped up by
the bedside lamp. "Gone for a walk. Don't wait breakfast
for me." That's all it said.

'Anyway, I got dressed and went down and had my
breakfast.' Flora paused, she was remembering, with guilt,
how she had enjoyed that breakfast on her own. Fergus
had, used to have, such an irritating way of attacking his
toast when he buttered it, scrunch, scrunch – set one's
nerves on edge, first thing in the morning.

'And then?'

'Then. Well. I finished my breakfast and I was just
crossing the hall when Mrs Lindsay popped out from her
office behind the reception desk and asked me if I could
spare her a minute.' Flora turned a wondering look on
Stella. 'Now wasn't that an odd thing to say – "Could
you spare me a minute, Mrs Sinclair?" – when she was
about to tell me that they'd just fished poor Fergus out of
the harbour?

'Mr Syme was in the office and a policeman. He'd seen Fergus fall in – Mr Syme, I mean. He goes for a swim early in the morning. He was on his way back when he spotted Fergus standing on top of the harbour wall – at the far end, the mouth of the harbour. He said he thought it was a dangerous place to be standing because the wind was gusting a bit off the land . . . well, I suppose people always say things like that, afterwards. In fact he didn't actually *see* Fergus fall in; he'd looked away for a second and when he glanced back towards Fergus, he'd gone. Just like that!'

Stella placed a hand over Flora's.

'It must have been very quick for him.'

'Very quick. Apparently he'd knocked his head on a rock so he wouldn't even have started to swim – the sea just took him. Perhaps he slipped, they're always slippery, aren't they, harbours? I did wonder if he might have staggered, lost his balance for a moment. The accident could have left him prone to dizziness. I thought he'd swayed a bit when he'd bent to tie up a shoelace when we were out on the golf course the day before. One goes over things in one's mind, you know, trying to find a cause, a reason – silly, really.'

'What accident was that?'

'The one with Eleanor, of course! That's why we came up here for a little break. I think Fergus wanted to put it behind him. Something like that.'

'Well, it's the first I've heard of an accident!'

'But of course – I'd forgotten you didn't know about it. Well, it wasn't much really.' Flora paused; she was tired of explaining, of recounting. Apart from answering a few questions at the inquest she hadn't had to tell anyone about the circumstances of Fergus's death – not until now. Certainly everyone in the hotel knows about it, probably everyone in Tangie Bay, come to that. I should be grateful really, it must be awful to have to keep talking about it, explain things, to people who don't already know. I'll have to get down to writing letters one day, Reggie Lomas, Mr Hazel, Eleanor . . . oh God! Why do people imagine it helps to talk about things; reducing events to words doesn't make things any more understandable. Stella's so calm, so detached; or seems to be. But then she probably imagines that I'm just as collected. What is she still looking so expectant about? Of course, the accident. She's waiting for me to tell her about that too.

Briefly, Flora outlined what had happened on the night when Fergus and Eleanor had driven away together from the pub.

Mrs Lindsay came in carrying a tea tray just as Flora finished speaking. 'There we are now!' she said, placing the tray on the table with an air of gentle solicitude that suggested she was bringing nourishment to a convalescent. 'I'm that glad you're here at last, Miss Sinclair. There's nothing like having your own folk around you at a time like this. Mind you, she's been real brave! Now,

Miss Sinclair, you see to it that she eats up her tea, like a good lassie. She needs to keep up her strength.'

Tears of exasperation welled up in Flora's eyes. You've been my friend, Jenny Lindsay, she longed to protest, we've been two grown women together; you've lent me your strength through the numbed hours. Why now do you talk over my head to Stella as though I were a half-wit or a child? Is this an indignity that the bereaved have also to suffer – a collusion between the comforters, a sort of complicity which excludes the object of their comfort?

Mistaking the nature of the tears that stood in Flora's eyes, Mrs Lindsay patted her arm.

'You just put yourself outside some of that short-bread, my dear, and you'll soon be feeling as right as rain! I'll be leaving you to get on with it then,' she added with a conspiratorial little nod and a smile in Stella's direction.

'She means well,' said Stella drily, when the door had closed, carefully and almost silently, behind Mrs Lindsay.

'She really has been awfully kind,' said Flora, charitably reminding herself that that had indeed been the case.

'Golly! There's enough here to feed a regiment!' Stella was looking with some awe at the tray, laden with plates of pancakes, scones, toast oozing with honey, little cakes with paper jackets.

'I know, I know! They all keep telling me that I must eat. You'd think I was pregnant and "eating for two". It's

so daft . . . because now I really am only one, one, one!'
Flora laughed but stopped herself as she became aware of
an hysterical edge to the sound.

'That night – you know, when Fergus was in Eleanor's
car – was he drunk too?'

'Tight as a tick!' said Flora, lightly. She was praying
that Stella would not ask why Fergus had gone on a
blinder. No point in distressing Stella by raking over
that business about his fish. She might even feel guilty
and that, surely, wouldn't be fair.

'It does occur to me – you know how he liked to play
the gallant – do you suppose that perhaps it could have
been Fergus who was driving and not Eleanor?'

Flora, as Stella was quick to notice, did not seem startled by her suggestion. But neither did she answer the
question; instead she posed another.

'But it was Eleanor herself who said she had been driving. Why ever would she tell the police that, if it wasn't
true?' Flora kept her eyes on her plate as though she were
indeed intent on obeying Mrs Lindsay's instructions to
eat up like a good girl. 'I'm sticking to my guns,' Eleanor
had said, she recalled as she spread jam with meticulous
care all over her shortbread.

'Oh, I don't know. It may have amused her to do
something quixotic, or perhaps she wanted to place
Fergus under a sense of obligation. Who knows? She is
a very odd sort of person, after all. Gracious, Flora!
What are you doing? I've never seen anyone put jam on

shortbread before – think of the calories, for heaven's sake!'

Suddenly Stella gave a little shriek and leapt up from the table. 'Damn!' she cried, rushing to the washbasin and scrubbing with a damp facecloth at the smear of honey which had trickled on to her skirt.

If, thought Flora, staring dully at the mess on her own plate, if Fergus had allowed Eleanor to take the blame, had had to face that he was capable of letting such a thing happen . . . no, I won't even think about it; certainly not now, after all, I've avoided thinking about it before. Poor Fergus, always so eager to blame his shortcomings on someone or something else; what would it have done to his self-respect if he had permitted someone else to voluntarily take the blame for something which was his responsibility?

'Oh, Stella – what a mess!'

'Not to worry! It's come out beautifully. The trick is to tackle it right away, not to give it time to soak in.'

They took a walk after tea. By mutual, although unspoken, consent they headed inland along a rutted farm road, leaving the village and its harbour behind them.

The heavy rain had ceased, but Mrs Lindsay, declaring that another downpour was in the offing, had insisted upon lending Stella a voluminous electric-blue raincoat, wellington boots and a large black funereal umbrella – an outfit which provided more than adequate protection from the fine soft drizzle that caressed their skin and spangled their hair with a cobweb mist.

'It may be difficult to believe, but we did have some really glorious days, Autumn's last fling, I suppose.' Flora was looking out over the sad, dun-coloured landscape that stretched monotonously flat to the foot of the hills that loomed indistinctly on the skyline. They had paused by a field-gate. Behind it, churned mud sucking at their hooves as they jostled gently for position, a herd of cows crowded, heavy uddered, bony haunched, patiently waiting to be collected for the evening milking.

For the most part, they walked in companionable silence, picking their way with care round the pot-holes, holding hands to steady themselves over the slippery slicks of mud. They skirted a field of swedes, the air heavy with the reek of the swollen roots, dull purple and ochre yellow, that awaited the onslaught of the sheep who would soon be brought down from the hills to weather the coming frosts and snow.

All this ought to depress me, thought Flora, glancing up at the leaden sky where peewits swooped and cried plaintively over the distant fields of barley stubble. But in spite of it all, I don't feel overwhelmed with gloom. This is only a season in a cycle, the seasons pass but the cycle continues.

The track ended in a farmyard. At its entrance stood a rowan tree, stunted and twisted by the winds from the sea. Its branches were filled with a gaggle of quarrelling

starlings tearing greedily at the berries that were clus-
tered, the last bright rags of Summer, among leaves
already changing colour.

A woman stood in the cobbled yard, a potato sack over
her shoulders, plump bare legs mauve with the cold. She
was scattering grain to a flock of damp and bedraggled hens
that clucked crossly round her feet. The paint on the byre
doors had faded to a gentle rose-madder tint, and a thin,
wiry old fellow in a black oilskin was swinging them open.

'Better get back before the cows block the road,' suggested Stella.

'You'd have to be strong to survive a life spent here,'
said Flora, with a backward glance at the woman in the
yard who had tossed the last of the grain high in the air
and was heading for the back door of the dour little
farmhouse. How can she bear it? Flora wondered, conscious of feeling guilty over her sense of dissatisfaction
with her own life whose exigencies must, by comparison,
seem relatively trivial.

'Strong or not, everyone just has to get on with living
as best they may. Every life has its own particular blood-
iness.' said Stella. Suddenly she jumped, both feet
together, into the middle of a large puddle.

'I've been longing to do that!' She looked down at Mrs
Lindsay's boots, now gleaming black. 'Got the mud and
the muck off, too.'

She looked so freakish, the arms of the raincoat flap-
ping over her hands, the too-large wellingtons, her hair

hanging in damp strands where the drizzle had insinuated itself under the rakish angle of the umbrella. Impulsively, Flora gave her a quick hug.

'I wish you could see yourself – you're such a fright! "Stella's Style" indeed! I shouldn't think the new line will catch on, dear.'

'Oh, I don't know – you must admit it has a certain *je ne sais quoi*! But Flora, why on earth did you have to come here in *October*, I *ask* you. One of these days, I'm going to take you on a super holiday, we'll go where the sun shines. Give me the sun, the sun!' Stella flung her arms wide and executed an outlandish pirouette and, miscalculating the length of her borrowed boots, trapped one toe under the other and would have fallen in the mud if Flora had not caught her. They staggered for a moment together under the darkening sky. The umbrella broke free and bowled down the track like a crippled bat of nightmare proportions before it veered into a bramble thicket where it came to rest.

Flora, running after Stella, felt light and free, the laughter, the childish fooling, acting like a catharsis. This feeling won't last, she warned herself, catching up with Stella and helping her to free the umbrella from the clutch of the brambles. It is like the shafts of optimism which come upon me and persuade me that there simply must be something better lying in wait; they pass too. But that is no reason why I should not relish them when they occur. Time may have filched away too many years, but that is all the more reason why I should make the most of those that are left.

'Did Fergus tell you that this was the room which Mother always had?' asked Stella when they were back at the hotel, their stockings washed and hung to dry on the towel rail, slippers on their feet and their faces still tingling and pink from rain and wind.

'No. Perhaps he didn't remember.'

'He must have. It looked a bit different then, of course, but the view hasn't changed at all.' Stella paused in the act of drawing the curtains shut and peered out over the golf course. The white painted woodwork of the little clubhouse's fretted veranda gleamed palely in the gloaming, inappropriately fanciful against the moorland backdrop.

'She always said that that – the clubhouse, I mean – reminded her of an Indian bungalow. Not that she'd ever been to India, but then her opinions were rarely informed. She did eventually go to India though – on a trip with that ghastly nurse creature, remember?' Stella rattled the curtains shut.

'There was only one bed in here in those days. A big double one between the windows, its back to the light, so convenient for reading in bed! She did a lot of that on rainy days or when she felt particularly fragile. Propped up on pillows with an Angela Thirkell or a Dornford Yates for solace. She just adored Dornford Yates – hence her sealyhams, I suppose. They'd be on the bed too, licking their bottoms and biting at the sheep ticks they'd picked up on the moor. Oh happy days!'

Stella glanced round the room and continued her comments on its changes.

Flora suspended the towelling of her hair to make her own quick survey of the bedroom, but what struck her were the changes which had been wrought in its appearance since the arrival of Stella. How, she wondered, could the contents of one small overnight bag be spread so far and create such untidy chaos where neat order had previously ruled? It was extraordinary how Stella, so organised and so patently efficient and successful in her business life, could be so very disorganised and careless in her private one.

'. . . a sort of trellis pattern of roses and forget-me-nots and there was a basketwork armchair just here and . . .' Stella broke off, realising that she had lost Flora's attention.

'Flora,' she said abruptly, as she sat down opposite her. 'I do understand how awful this has been for you, how awful it must still be. I know I'm not married, but I can still understand that Fergus was the other half of your life and now that he has gone you must feel like a sort of amputee. I know that perhaps I haven't said all the things expected of one in such circumstances; I don't think I've got much talent for – what's the word – condolences. They're so apt to sound like platitudes. That sort of thing embarrasses me, do you understand?'

Flora nodded; it embarrassed her too. Fergus's sudden death must have come as a shock to Stella, but she doubted whether it had meant more to her than just that. And as for herself? She was still, in a sense, trying to find Fergus. She was still not sure what he had meant to her or how his absence was going to affect her. Stella had said something about being an amputee – well, wasn't it the case that sudden loss of a part of one's body was dulled by a type of natural anaesthesia? Later that disappeared, and forever after, or so she understood, one was aware of pain in the limb that had been severed. A ghost limb, they called it. Oh Fergus, Fergus!

'But soon you must start thinking about the future, and perhaps that's where I can be of more help. What are you going to do with yourself now, Flora – have you given it any thought yet?'

'I have been turning it over in my mind, yes; but in a rather muddled sort of way. The snag is that I'm not really trained for any specific job. I can't think who might want to employ me.'

Busy once more towelling her hair, Flora did not see the look of surprise in Stella's face. It had not occurred to her that Flora might be thinking along the lines of a proper job. At her age, she thought, she must be mad!

'It's my own fault that I'm not qualified for much, I suppose,' Flora continued, emerging from the towel. 'I just gave up working in the last year at school. I was so utterly, madly in love with Fergus, you see. The need to qualify for a career . . . all that . . . just didn't make sense to me any more. I *knew* what I wanted.' Flora said it in a tone of wonder, still capable of surprising herself about herself.

'Failed my Highers – didn't give a damn! Daddy had wanted me to go on to train as a chemist, to sit my Highers again. "Get your back into it, life is not all beer and skittles, my girl!"' Flora giggled.

'I just let it all flow over me; must have been maddening for him, poor man! Oh, I was a disappointment to all of them. But not to Mother, though. As long as I didn't end up actually working behind the counter before Fergus led me to the altar, she was quite happy. I did agree to take a sort of half-baked commercial course so that I could do the books in the shop. Aunt Agnes was *appalled* – you can imagine. She tried to make me feel that I'd let down a whole generation of women who had striven for emancipation. All that. She told me that I'd "rue the day". But I don't think she'd have enjoyed seeing her prediction come true.'

Flora paused, still regretting the row she had had with her aunt, the only serious quarrel she could ever remember having had with her. 'Such a silly pointless waste – well, I suppose everything is that in the end, pointless!' Flora was remembering the manner in which her aunt had met her death. She'd been knocked off her bicycle by a reeling drunk in the wartime blackout and thrown in the path of an army truck.

'Oh for heavens sake, Flora! I don't think nihilism really suits you at all!'

'No? Well no, of course not. All I'm saying is that I was a bit of a silly fool at a crucial stage. Anyway, girls didn't think so much about careers then. Some did, but lots of us were just looking for a stop-gap until Mr Right came along.'

She brushed aside Stella's protestation.

'Oh I know that *you* were determined on a proper career. But you were that much younger, you see. How old were you when the war started – barely eleven? I think it was the war and all the opportunities that it opened up that made girls grow keener on getting on in their own right. Attitudes changed. In the end, though, I don't suppose I can blame anyone but myself – I just fluffed my chances!'

Flora shook out her towel and draped it neatly over a radiator.

'But I'm determined now that I'm not going to just drift along any longer. And one thing I'm *not* going to do is to go back to Hillcrest to moulder on my own! Even supposing that I could afford to – which I can't.'

'Good for you! Look, Flora, I was turning a plan over in my mind even while I was coming up here. I think you should come and live with me.'

'Oh, no Stella, you mustn't feel obliged to . . . there's no need, really. Anyway, I couldn't . . .'

'No, don't get me wrong. You see, you'd be doing *me*

a service. Just listen a minute. A friend of mine is selling me her house – it's a lovely little place near the Embankment and I've been longing to get out of my flat. But the thing is, I really need someone reliable and competent to look after it. To look after me, too, I suppose! Someone to take all the domestic worries off me, to leave me free for *my* job, d'you see?'

That sounded a familiar proposition, thought Flora, but expressed more honestly than it generally was.

Stella was leaning forward, hands outstretched, voice eager. Her enthusiasm for her plan was genuine, born as it was of a long and painful tussle with a succession of housekeepers: Spanish, Nordic, French – Stella, as she had frequently said (although not to Flora), could write a book about her horrendous experiences with domestic helpers. It was not, as she would point out – it not seeming to occur to her listeners to do so – it was not as though she were unreasonable or expected altogether too much from her staff!

'There's even a garden. Tiny, of course, but enough for you to grow herbs. You are such a superb cook, Flora. Oh yes, you are! I plan to do more of my business entertaining at home, much more intimate, you know. You could look after all that sort of thing. It would be a proper job – *your* job! And then, when I have to go abroad, you'd be able to come with me and look after all the little details so that I'd be free to concentrate on the business side of things. I just *know* you'd do it wonderfully well.

171

You were absolutely wasted on Fergus, you know . . .'
Hastily, she added, 'And we get on so marvellously
together, don't we? I am sure it would work beautifully,
Flora!'

But Flora had ceased to listen too closely to the torrent
of words. She had a vision of terracotta pots on a doll's
house patio, pots filled with basil, marjoram, thyme; one
of those fiddly little watering cans that look like a child's
toy standing nearby. Herself ironing Stella's blouses, pol-
ishing wine glasses, screwing the lids back on cosmetic
jars. Waiting for the sound of the key in the lock, pouring the reviving martini for the returned worker . . .
'Flora thinks of everything!'. No, that was Letty.

'Stella, it's awfully good of you to make me such an
offer, but I really don't think . . .'

Stella leapt up and placed her fingers on Flora's lips.

'No, no! Not a word, darling! Not yet. You've got to
have time to think about it. I don't want to rush you.
Tomorrow afternoon you'll fly back to London with me
and then you'll need to return to Hillcrest for a few days
to pack up there and attend to all the bits and pieces; see
your solicitor about Fergus's affairs – all that sort of
thing. As soon as I possibly can, I'll wangle a few days
free to come down and we'll tie this thing up together.
But not a word more about it now, promise?' Stella
glanced at her watch. 'My God! Nearly time for dinner.
I must make a call to my secretary first.'

'Won't the office be closed by now?'

'Oh, I'll get her at home, she's quite used to that! I'll tell you what – while I'm ringing her, would you be an angel and run my bath before someone else bags the bathroom? Oh, and there's a travelling iron somewhere or other amongst my things, so if you want to use it on anything just you go ahead. My blouse could do with a freshening up – but only if you're going to do some ironing anyway.' She planted a quick kiss on Flora's forehead.

'Keep yourself busy, darling, that's much the best thing!'

'If I'd known the dinner was going to be so lousy, I'd have stoked up on that enormous afternoon tea.' Stella was sitting up in bed massaging cream into her hands.

'Ah, but what's served downstairs bears no comparison to what Mrs Lindsay brought to us; I told you, she's singled me out for special privileged treatment.'

'Bed's comfortable enough. That's something.'

'I nearly forgot – you haven't seen this yet.' Flora took a newspaper cutting from her bedside table and handed it across the intervening space to Stella.

'My goodness!' Stella, in mock-melodramatic tones, read the headline aloud: '"Hero of pre-war sea rescue drowns in Tangie Bay". They've even reprinted all the guff the local paper printed at the time, how extraordinary! I mean to say, all that was years ago – how did they make the connection?'

'I think Mrs Lindsay must have spoken to the reporter. They would have been bound to have sent someone round to the hotel. I expect death by drowning is rated big news by the locals. Mrs Lindsay's husband was drowned too, during the war. There's a bit about that at the end of the article, under the heading: "Strange Coincidence"!'

'Mmm.' Stella's eyes were racing cursorily over the text. 'Fergus would have been frightfully chuffed!'

How did people know with such certainty what would have pleased the dead? Not so long ago, hadn't Stella suggested that perhaps he wished the incident at the Daisy Rock had never happened, that he wanted to forget it. And now she was sure he would like to have his act of bravery remembered. How could people presume to know such things? But I expect I will start doing the same sort of thing myself, thought Flora. Fergus is mine now, in a way he never was in life; mine to do with as I please. I can begin to pretend now that I really understood him, knew him. I may even, in time, reconstruct him in an image of my own choosing. She suspected that the widows wintering in The Golf View were doing just that when they spoke to one another of their dead spouses: 'yes, he was one in a thousand', 'always so cheerful, a great one for a lark, my George was', 'such a demon for work, too conscientious really, I always think that's what killed the dear man in the end!' Oh yes, she'd heard them at it in the lounge, twittering one to the other over the teacups. It was surprising how many people improved after death. But Flora admitted to herself that she had felt childishly pleased that they'd all read the newspaper article – Mrs Lindsay having drawn their attention to it.

The paper was stained now with Stella's handcream. Flora folded it up and replaced it in the drawer without a second glance, as though it were of little account. But Stella wasn't watching her. She was already intent on the final rituals of bedtime: wiping her hands on a tissue, tossing back a sleeping pill, rearranging her pillows.

'Sleep well, darling. Night, night!' she said, clicking out her bedside light.

It was companionable, comforting, to have the second bed occupied. Its emptiness had been disturbing. It was strange, thought Flora, but that was all that Fergus had, at least so far, left behind him – a sense of his absence. A space unoccupied. She had expected to feel his presence still. But there was simply nothing. Not here, anyway; not in The Golf View. Perhaps Fergus was waiting for her in Hillcrest.

'Stella!' she whispered.

'What?' Stella's voice sounded already drowsy.

'There's something I'd like to talk about, something I want to ask you . . .'

'Not now, Flora. Remember we agreed we'd talk about plans when you'd had time to think things over – tomorrow, maybe.'

'It's nothing to do with future plants. It's . . . well, did you ever hear the expression "the sea will not be denied"?'

There, it had been said.

But no answer came from Stella. There was no sound at all from the other bed except for her light, steady breathing.

Flora switched off the lamp by her own bed and lay still; herself the only audience for the remembered story which Stella would now never hear. And that's just as well, thought Flora, glad now that Stella had fallen asleep before she could have confided it to her. She'd only have thought me crazy to think it worth recounting. Perhaps she would be right!

She recalled once more the circumstances in which she had heard that phrase, an incident so apparently inconsequential that it had lain buried, unexamined, in her mind for years until recent events had wrenched it from her unconscious mind. She had been vaguely aware that something struggled to come to the forefront of her memory when first Fergus had mentioned Jenny, Mrs Lindsay as she now was. Something had come to her then, a recollection of Mrs Davidson's niece as being one of a group of women seated round the kitchen table at Peepie Cottage. Jenny's presence remembered, perhaps, because she had been the only young person in that company; scarcely a woman but, like Flora herself at that time, a girl in her late teens.

It had been the evening of the exploit at the Daisy Rock. Mrs Munro had sent Flora to the kitchen to ask Mrs Davidson why the bedtime cocoa had not yet been brought in. In order to remind Mrs Davidson that a vigilant eye was being kept upon what went on in the kitchen of Peepie Cottage, Mrs Munro was in the habit of sending either Flora or the unsuspecting Annie on such errands. The payment made to Mrs Davidson covered not only the rental of the cottage but also included a sum in consideration of Mrs Davidson's services as cook and cleaner; but the food in the larder was all bought and paid for by Mrs Munro and she strongly suspected that these provisions were regularly plundered to provide refreshment for Mrs Davidson's cronies when they congregated of an evening in her kitchen to indulge in what Mrs Davidson described as 'a bit of a crack'.

That evening the kitchen had been more than usually crowded with Mrs Davidson's friends, all avid for more details of the rescue. The only account of that event as yet in circulation in the village was that of the two men who had witnessed it all from the clifftop path, and they, being typical of their sex, had failed to flesh out the story with the sort of telling details which only a woman could appreciate or provide. Mrs Davidson's version of what had occurred would obviously provide a far more enthralling story as it would be based upon information gleaned from the women who had been present and who had played their own part in the rescue.

177

Flora had paused for a moment outside the half-open kitchen door, dreading to enter and be exposed to the keen gaze of all those sharp eyes. The women, as usual, had their knitting with them, but Flora knew from previous observation that that circumstance would in no way prevent them from scrutinising her every move; the fishermen's pullovers and long-johns which grew with such astonishing speed under their flying fingers and flashing steel needles appeared to do so without benefit of visual supervision.

It was immediately apparent to Flora, as she peeped hesitantly round the edge of the door, that a row was about to erupt or had, indeed, already done so. Experienced as she was at detecting the atmosphere generated by female dissension, she recognised all too well the tell-tale tension that hung over the group of women seated round the table. One or two of them had actually ceased to ply their needles.

'Go you, like a good lassie, and fetch in a scuttle of coal for the morn!' Mrs Davidson, her colour raised, was saying to Jenny in a voice that brooked no argument.

But it was not towards young Jenny that her anger was directed. As soon as Jenny had risen from the table and, scuttle in hand, had obediently left the kitchen, Mrs Davidson had turned her attention, and her wrath, upon the old woman who was seated at the head of the table.

'Whatever are you thinking about, Bella Young! Coming out with that heathen superstition in front of the lassie. And in *my* kitchen! Y'ken fine enough that it was Jenny's Angus, and him her intended, that howked old Geordie Bain out of the harbour and now you go frightening her with that old nonsense. You should be proper ashamed of yourself, so you should.'

'I'll say what I want to say – in your kitchen Cissie Davidson or anywhere else I've a mind to! And forby it's true, and well you know it. The sea will not be denied! That's the way of it, whether you like it or not. Bide its time it may, but in the end . . . You mark my words, Cissie!'

'Will you no whisht now!' hissed Mrs Davidson as a bumping at the back door signified Jenny's return.

Flora moved restlessly in her bed, envious of Stella's calm sleep.

The full memory of what she had overheard but not comprehended on that far-off night had come to Flora when Jenny Lindsay, on the day of Fergus's death, had offered her as comfort the advice that one could not escape one's destiny. That what would happen in life, would happen, and that there was no profit to be gained by questioning the why or the wherefore. Jenny had murmured the injunction with such conviction that her words were lent a significance that outweighed the banality of the sentiment.

'My Angus and your Fergus, the both of them; it makes you wonder, and no mistake! As some would have it, you rob the sea at your peril,' she had added, placing her hand gently on Flora's shoulder.

Flora could not understand why the implication of a grim and primitive old wives' tale should provide a measure of comfort. But it did. It suggested, at least, an inevitability about what would befall one, and that seemed easier to accept than the suspicion that perhaps nothing ruled one's life at all other than random chance.

I can't bring myself to really believe it. But I wish I could. Perhaps I do. I don't really know what I believe any more, Flora admitted to herself. It all seems so easy, until something like this happens.

Flora turned over on her other side and made a conscious effort to relax her limbs, to silence her mind, to sleep. She could hear her wristwatch whispering time away. She must sleep because tomorrow she must waken early to do those things which had, as yet, been left undone.

10

~

Flora wondered if Stella had awakened yet and if she had found the note that Flora had left for her on the dressing table: 'Gone for a walk. Don't wait breakfast for me.'

She stood at the seaward end of the Daisy Rock. The tide was on the turn, the waves choppy, restless, petulantly slapping the rocks below her. Caught in the cross flow of the current, the thick stems of the submerged kelp twisted and writhed, their long leather thongs waving like pennants in a teasing wind.

The water looked dark and so bitterly cold, as though it was reluctant to admit the light of the freshly broken day. It was impossible to see where the sea ended and the sky began and even such light as shafted through the tattered scarves of morning mist held no promise of warmth to come but touched the waves with wands of chill steel.

Quailing in the face of such desolation, Flora turned her back upon the open sea before her resolution would be utterly undermined. The light westerly breeze had already swept the mist away from the land, and the sea, bound by the sweep of the shore, dwarfed by the cliffs that reared above it, lost its frightening air of implacable immensity.

A solitary oystercatcher ran energetically to and fro at the water's edge, probing with its orange-red beak at the dark sand laid freshly bare by the retreating waves. Flora stood for a little while looking down upon it, strangely comforted by its presence and air of purposefulness. In the strengthening light she could see its footprints etched in its wake for a brief space of time before the shifting grains of sand obliterated the delicate tracery so that no evidence remained to mark its busy passage.

Picking her way with care, Flora clambered down the side of the ridge to the jumble of rocks which were already exposed by the ebbing tide. In this happy hunting ground of childhood it seemed strange to be carrying not a bucket and spade but a bulky handbag. The rock pools were perhaps smaller than she remembered them, but their fascination was not diminished.

Flora folded the skirts of her coat tightly around her and seated herself on a flat barnacled rock. She stared down into the miniature sea that lay at her feet – an intimate, contained sea where anemones, fat and bright as jujubes, waved their tentacles, and tiny, translucent shrimp-like creatures crawled through the fronds of russet and green wrack.

It looked so permanent, that little world with its self-absorbed inhabitants going about their various activities; dozing, fighting, copulating, eating one another up. But before nightfall the sea would crash over it, scattering its occupants, both destroying and renewing their habitat. The behaviour of the waves would owe nothing to caprice. Their return would be at the time appointed by the pattern of the tide. But what could the starfish, the anemones or any of the occupants of the pool know or understand of the existence of laws that both ordered and disrupted their lives?

Opening her bag, Flora took from it a square, varnished wooden box. She lifted the lid and leaned over the pool.

Alerted perhaps by the movement above it, a crab that had lurked undetected on the floor of the pool raised itself up on the points of its claws and scurried sideways seeking the shelter of a clump of seaweed. The weed, fine as hair, trembled in the water as the crab settled itself down to crouch, still as a stone, under its cover, waiting for whatever sustenance might come its way.

Flora drew back her hand and snapped shut the lid of the box. Dust to dust was one thing – but who could predict the ultimate destiny of that scavenging crab!

It was, Flora discovered, more difficult to climb back up the side of the Daisy Rock than it had been to descend. Suddenly afraid that she might slip backwards into the sea, she tackled the last few yards of the ascent on hands and knees. Once safely back on the ridge, she sank down on the sparse wiry grass to recover her breath and quieten the flutter of panic that had so unexpectedly overtaken her.

As she put down her bag, its strap detached itself on one side. She remembered that Fergus had repaired it for her with a smear of glue and a measure of optimism. 'It'll hold for the time being,' he had said.

Along the beach from the direction of the village, a figure was approaching at a leisurely lope. Instantly recognisable in his pea-green tracksuit, Mr Syme came inexorably nearer as Flora threw herself forward on her elbows in the fervent hope that she would remain unobserved.

He came to a halt in the lee of a rock, unrolled the striped towel which had been tucked under one arm and shook out the bathing trunks which it had held.

Oh my God, he's going to undress for his morning swim! I ought to look the other way, or at least close my eyes, Flora told herself. Even when crouched like a camel on a windswept rock, one ought to observe the decencies, she chided herself as she watched Mr Syme remove his running shoes and socks. But what happened next was not at all what she expected.

Mr Syme walked briskly down to the water's edge, dipped his bathing trunks in the sea, sluiced some water over his head and trotted back to his rock. He quickly dried his feet, replaced his socks and shoes and, finally, wrapped up his sopping wet trunks inside his towel.

Flora scrambled to her feet as Mr Syme turned his back on the Daisy Rock and began to walk back to Tangie Bay at a pace which would doubtless quicken to a jog as he approached Harbour Street.

She stood for a moment, watching with wry amusement tinged with compassion the slowly dwindling figure on the beach. There goes another one, she thought, playing games, pretending, getting through life as best he can.

Flora stooped to retrieve her bag from where it lay on a clump of thrift as plump and rounded as a foot-stool. It was the thrift, the sea daisy, that grew in such abundance along its crest, that gave the Daisy Rock its name. She took the box from her bag and dropped once more to her knees. Gently she lifted up the cushion of growth that rested on stone, anchored there by one wiry root at its heart. The root had insinuated itself into a crevice in the rock and there held fast, continuing to grow and live out its life in defiance of all the odds.

Carefully she let the ashes from the box flow around the root of the plant and trickle down into the fissure in the rock. Tenderly she pressed the mat of foliage back into its accustomed position. The grey-pink flowers were now no more than dried rustling heads still clinging stubbornly to their stems, above the reach of even the highest of tides.

Quickly she strode once more to the furthest point of the Daisy Rock and flung the empty box out to sea. There it bobbed, almost jauntily on the crest of a wave.

Like a little ship, Flora thought, as it rode further and further from her gaze on waves that sparkled now in the clear light of day.

Flora stood quite still, listening to the sound of the sea, breathing in its tang, watching the little speck on the water until it disappeared from sight.

Now, she reminded herself, there are decisions to be made, her future to be considered.

She could debate, ponder and consider what best to do.

Or she could adopt her aunt's philosophy and be content to 'trust the future to His providence'.

Either way, the outcome would certainly be beyond her control, but not, perhaps, other than it was destined to be.

She stooped and plucked at random a handful of the stiff wiry stems that still carried the withered daisies of Summer and tossed them from her, one by one, into the sea below. As they dropped in turn to the water she murmured, 'yes, no.'

'Yes!' she said, as the last stem left her fingers.

So, it was to be life with Stella. Well, she reflected, it may work out quite satisfactorily.

At any rate, Flora told herself as she turned her back on the sea, I can give it a try – pro tem.